Rivers

Book Two

Through the Eyes of a Blind Dog

Mike Dillingham

PO Box 221974 Anchorage, Alaska 99522-1974

ISBN 1-59433-004-2

Library of Congress Catalog Card Number: 2003111941

Manufactured in the United States of America.

Dedication

To my wife Mary, who made it possible for me to write this book.

To my friends, who encourage me.

To my dogs, who give me their unconditional love.

To Rivers, whose courage and energy inspires me.

In memory of Rivers' trail buddies, who are now at rest.

And finally, in loving memory of Sandy, our fun loving, coffee drinking, and devoted housedog, 1990 to 2003.

Cast of Critters

Rivers

Sandy

Christmas

Sky

Stormy

Tundra

Mike, Rivers, and Fin

Lakota

Doc

Ugly

Nitro

Brownie

Aurora

Sunny

Table of Content

Photo Credits

All photos used with permission.
Cast of Critters Page: Christmas (AKA, Ice) - photo by the Richeys,
Tracks of Alaska; Mike, Fin, and Rivers - photo by the Richeys, Tracks
of Alaska; Aurora Gooddog (AKA, Kobuk) - GB Jones; Sunny (AKA,
Chena) - Donna Quante, Husky lover; all other Cast of Critters photos
by Mike and Mary Dillingham. Forward Page: photo by the Richeys,
Tracks of Alaska; Rivers' Page: photo by the Richeys, Tracks of Alaska,
Back Cover: Mike and Rivers - photo by the Richeys, Tracks of Alaska.

8

Acknowledgments

Doctor Jim Gaarder DVM/ DACVO who cared for Sandy and Rivers as if they were his own dogs. Doctor Jim also provided the technical insight I needed for this book.

Stan Smith, Iditarod 1993 and 1994. Stan lit my sled dog fire with his vivid descriptions of his adventures on the trail. He provided a great deal of technical advice and pointed me in the right direction when I trained my dogs.

The Richeys, who were responsible for many of the photos used in this book and on our web site. To view more of the Richey's pictures, please check out their web site at http://www.tracksofalaska.com/

Becky and Bob at "Dog Duds: Custom Sewing for Canines and Their Humans" who made all of the booties we use.

Mike Fisher of Lost Creek General Services. Mike made our training scooter, while his wife Diane, who is an avid Rivers' fan, runs her "Fluff Team" on the Oregon sand dunes. Please visit Mike at http://www.trainingcarts.com/

GB Jones, Iditarod 2002 and 2003. GB taught me how to mush and trusted me with his dogs and sled. He searched for my dogs when they were lost and constantly told us we would find them, which we did after 9 days. GB has a nice web site at http://www.alaskanmusher.com

Mark, at The Grateful Sled, who hand made the sled we use.

My test readers, Barbara, Bonnie, Dawn and her son Joe, Edna ("Rivers biggest fan in the Northwest") Doug and Rosemary, thank you. Rosemary used the original "Rivers" manuscript to help her students overcome their individual challenges. The "PS

49" chapter in my first book, "Rivers, Diary of a Blind Alaska Racing Sled Dog" is dedicated to Rosemary and her students. And of course, our good friend Margie.

Evan Swensen, my publisher, of Publications Consultants. Without Evan's help, support, encouragement, and guidance, none of the Rivers books would have made a difference in the lives of so many. Evan has helped authors throughout Alaska produce great books about Alaska. Check out Evan's Webs site at http://www.alaskabooks.biz/

The dogs. I would be remiss if I did not acknowledge the dogs, not only my own, but all of the ones that I met during my travels. All of their nose licks, paw shakes, and their TLC are embedded within these pages.

Our friends at the Wasilla Veterinary Clinic who care for all our fur buddies as if they were their own.

Foreword

Rivers is a real live dog who lives with my family in Palmer, Alaska. Working with Rivers has changed my life in more positive ways than I could ever have imagined. Every day, we receive e-mail from children and adults who tell us that Rivers' stories have inspired or motivated them.

I have watched Rivers grow from a lonely kennel dog to a loving, playful companion. Rivers' learning ability, courage, and unstoppable desire to run the trails continue to amaze me. He has become one of my heroes. I hope he becomes one of yours also.

Rivers' Note

Mike is a very good storyteller. So while I am a real live dog, some of the adventures and characters in this book are, well "Tales of the trails, from wagging tails." I hope you enjoy our adventures and visit us on our web site at http:/home.gci.net/ ~sleddog or email me at rivers@rogershsa.com

See Ya!
RIVERS

Letter of Introduction

Rosemary Parker
Special Education 4th Grade Teacher
PS 49 in Queens New York

Who would have ever guessed that a chance encounter 3 years ago on the Blinddogs e-mail site would bring together a New York City Special Education Teacher and an author from Alaska (a former New Yorker from Astoria, Queens)?

As Mike Dillingham and I exchanged stories about our blind dogs, Rivers and my Dalmatian Asia, (who is now at the Rainbow Bridge) we never imagined the impact Rivers would have on my Special Needs class.

I test read Mike's first book to my class and they immediately fell in love with Rivers. Through Rivers' bravery and courage in spite of his handicap, my class made a connection. They found faith in themselves to succeed using Rivers as their role model. They wrote letters to Rivers who wrote back to them.

Through Mike's and his wife Mary's generosity, (they sent them books, buttons, maps, videos and weekly updates from Rivers) my class was motivated and inspired to work hard. I did many literacy lessons using Rivers, his book and the Iditarod as a theme. Guess what happened... their reading and writing improved as well as their outlook. The kids wanted to give back to Rivers so one year they did a Bake Sale to raise money for Rivers' former musher. The next year they did the same for the IMOM group (who helped Rivers get his surgery). They raised over $600 for sick animals whose owners could not afford medical care for them.

Rivers has touched their lives and hearts tremendously. They will always bring a piece of him with them for the rest of their lives. Mike and Rivers made that happen for them.

Mike's Christmas Wish

2001 Christmas Story

"Wake up Rivers."

I heard the voice, but I must have been dreaming. "Wake up, Rivers," the voice said again. I opened my eyes. Yes, blind dogs do close their eyes when they sleep. When I opened my eyes, I saw a beautiful dog glowing with a soft light that filled my doghouse with warmth.

Wait a minute, I cannot see. This must be a dream. Looks like a good one, I thought, as I asked, "Who are you?"

"My name is Aurora Gooddog and I was sent here to grant your buddy Mike his Christmas wish," she said.

Yes, it was Christmas time again and I remembered last year when I was so worried because I did not have a gift for Mike. However, last Christmas Eve, the guys and I found a little puppy and saved her. Mike told us that he was very happy and proud of what we did and it was a great present to give him. We showed him that we cared about others. It felt great to give Mike something. He has given me so much, for which I am very grateful.

However, again this year I had nothing to give him. Aurora's voice got my attention. "You know, Rivers, for a smart dog you think way too much. I know what you are thinking. You forget that dogs give their buddies presents all year long. You give your obedience, your loyalty, and your love. See, Rivers," Aurora said, "dogs don't need special days to give presents. We give them everyday. Moreover, according to my records, you and your teammates do a great job of that. So Rivers, you gave Mike some super presents all year."

Her words made sense and I felt a lot better. Yes, Aurora is right, I do think too much. "Yes you are right." I said. "But what is this thing about your coming here to grant Mike his Christmas wish?"

"Well, it seems that your buddy Mike has some friends in very high places, She said. "However, we cannot do it."

I guess I got a little feisty. Mike deserved to have his wish granted. "Wait a minute, that is not fair." I demanded, "Why can't Mike have his wish granted?"

"His wish is not for himself," Aurora answered. "His wish is for you to see, and that is impossible. Well, it is not impossible; it is impractical. You have no eyeballs and if all of a sudden you could see, a lot of humans would ask too many questions."

"Yes," I said sadly, "I understand." If people knew that a blind dog led a team in the last big race, there would have been a lot of trouble.

"They told me you were a smart dog; they sure are right." Aurora said. "But I am here to offer you a deal. I have the power to let you see for one day and one day only," she said. "Unfortunately, you can't tell anyone you can see, or act like you can see. You will have one day to take in all of the sights and keep those memories close to your heart. Mike has some special stuff planned for you and the team, so you will see the best that humanity has to offer." I listened as Aurora continued, "Nevertheless, there is a downside and that is it may be cruel to do this for you."

I was about to ask what she was talking about when she said, "You spent years overcoming your loss of vision and accepting being blind. It could be very hard for you to see for one day and then go back to the darkness. Also," she continued, "Mike can never know this happened. You may think that it is not fair to him, but he has plenty of faith and... well, just leave it with that."

"Now Rivers, you have to make a decision." Yes, a tough one too, I thought. Do I choose to see for one only day? On the other hand, do I choose not to see, and wonder what I am missing? I could see Mike, my buddies, and little Christmas, the puppy we saved last year. I could see the chow I get to eat and the house I sleep in. I could see the trail I run on and the snow. There is no choice. It has to be yes!

"Yes!" I said, "I want to see, if only for the one day. I want the memories." I pleaded, "Please Aurora, let me see."

"Okay, Aurora said. "You will see, but remember the rules." She continued, "If you break the rules, then what you see, and their memories will be erased from your heart and mind forever. Agreed?" She asked.

"Yes," I said. "I agree."

Then she told me, "Go back to sleep. When you wake, you will see. You will be up before any of your buddies. Your other senses will be as strong as they are now, so you will need some time to adjust to the difference."

When Aurora said, "Go to sleep," I laid my head down and dozed off. When I woke up, I thought, that was some dream I had. Wow, it sure is bright. Wait a minute. It sure is bright. I turned my head and.... I could see! It was not a dream. Mike got his wish and I could see! I jumped up and raced out of my doghouse. I looked around the yard. I saw my buddies' dog-houses painted green and each with a big yellow sign with their names on them. I looked around and I saw the big house where Mike and Mary live. There were Christmas lights and a big Santa with a sled and reindeer on the roof. Lakota told me all about the decorations last year. There was the warming shed and the garage where Mike keeps the trucks. And snow! Yes, I remember seeing many of these things before I went blind. And the sunrise! Oh, wow, how beautiful!

My buddies started to get up. "Morning, Rivers." It was Lakota. He is a lot bigger than I thought he was. Big paws! He looked so strong and somewhat sad.

"Hi Lakota". I said.

"Boy, Rivers, you sure sound happy this morning," Lakota said.

"Oh?" I said. "Well this is Christmas Day and I am happy for all the joy and happiness that will happen today."

"Merry Christmas, Rivers," Lakota answered.

As each of my teammates came out of their doghouses, I greeted them and took a very good look at them. There was Doc, the smart one with blue eyes. He is smaller than I imagined. Next to Doc was Nitro, the biggest dog on our team and brave too. Then I saw Brownie, who is three or four shades of brown. Next, I saw Ugly, who is a real handsome dog. He is the clown of our team.

"Morning, Uncle Rivers." It was little Christmas, who really is not little any more. She is over a year old. Her eyes are blue and she always looks like she is smiling. She is a very beautiful dog.

"How are you doing this morning, Christmas?" I asked.

"I am so excited Uncle Rivers," she said. "Mike said I can be the lead dog today. I heard him saying that we are going over to the orphanage to give some goodies to the poor kids there."

Yes, I remembered that also. This was sure going to be a fun day. Christmas scampered off to play with her other uncles. I sat

there, just looking at everything. I wanted to remember everything I saw and not waste a precious second of this great day.

"Yo, Rivey buddy." I looked in the direction of the voice and there was Mike with Sandy. Yes, I would know that voice anywhere, so I knew it had to be Mike. I watched him as he walked over toward me. I saw his beard and the glasses that I tend to knock off his face when I jump up to greet him. He has a slight limp. Mike is not as big as I imagined.

Sandy looked just like I pictured her, a chunky yellow lab, with a lot of gray in her face. Nevertheless, she was still very pretty and looked strong. While she sure was bossy and sassy, we all knew she is kind and was very devoted to Mike.

It was sure hard to just sit there until Mike came over. I had to act as if I was still blind. When I saw his hands reach out to pet me, I jumped up to him as I normally do and nuzzled Mike's beard. "Well buddy, you sure are affectionate this morning." He chuckled, "You got the Christmas spirit, I bet." Yes sir, Mike, no doubt about that.

I watched Mike give all of the guys a lot of TLC (Tender Loving Care) and then enjoyed watching Ugly play his normal chase game with Christmas. She would tease him and then he would run after her. She would hide behind Mike and Ugly would have to stop short or else run into Mike. Sometimes Mike would jump out of the way and then Christmas would have to run to get away from Ugly. This was very funny to watch. I always pictured it in my mind, but Christmas was just a little puppy and Ugly was a big dog. Actually, Christmas is taller than Ugly.

I started to laugh. "What are you laughing about Rivers?" It was Doc. Now I had to be careful round him because he is so smart and sensitive, he would know something was different.

"Christmas and Ugly are playing their chase game, right Doc?" I asked.

"Yes, and it is sure funny to watch."

I replied, "I bet it is, I can picture it in my mind." I knew Doc felt bad because I could not see them play.

"Want me to describe it to you, Rivers?" He asked.

"Nah," I said, "I can imagine what they look like. Thanks anyway." I saw him turn and walk away to talk to Brownie and Nitro.

Soon it was chow time, and Mike had a big shiny bucket steaming with good smells. I watched him make his rounds filling our dog bowls up with hot chow. When he got to me, I

looked at the bucket and saw myself in its reflection. So, that is what I look like! I never knew since I had never seen myself. Nitro was right last year when he said that Christmas and I have the same markings.

The chow was better than normal, or was it because I could actually see what I was eating for a change? Christmas always comes over to me to push the crumbs of kibble I drop back into my bowl. Hmmm. I had better drop some crumbs so she does not catch on that I can see. I can look right into her face. I could not believe how blue her eyes were.

Soon after we finished eating, Mike came out of the house in a red suit with a lot of white fur on it. His beard seemed a lot longer and was snow white. He also looked a lot fatter. I mean a lot fatter. I heard Brownie laugh and say that Mike was dressed up like the big Santa on the top of the house. I looked up at the Santa on the roof and Brownie was right. Mike and Santa look a lot alike. Sure makes you wonder, right?

I watched Mike get our sled and harnesses out of the warming shed. The guys had described these things to me. The sled was medium size and its wooden parts were very shiny. The gang, tug, and necklines were all the same color green as our collars. We all had green harnesses with our names on them. Mike then got a big bag stuffed with things wrapped in colored paper and placed it in the sled basket.

As he hooked us up to the sled, he told us that we were going to the orphanage to deliver gifts to the poor kids. Since it was such a beautiful day, Mike hoped that the kids could play outside with us. Mike said that some of the kids had never played with a dog before. Well, I know there are seven of us who are happy to play with those kids. Excuse me, eight of us. Mike was putting a harness on Sandy. Great! Sandy would go with us. Surprisingly, she was not putting up a fuss as she normally did. If you ask her, she is the housedog, not a sled dog.

We were ready to go. Christmas was the lead dog and Mike let me be the co-lead. He had done that before. Doc and Lakota were the swing dogs. Brownie and Ugly came next with Nitro and Sandy in the rear or wheel position. We were about ready to leave our yard when Mary came out of the house. She said she had a camera and wanted to take pictures of us.

Then Mike said, "On Christmas, On Rivers. On Doc and Lakota. On Ugly, On Brownie. On Nitro and Sandy."

"Oh stop clowning around Mike, and let me get your picture." Mary said, laughing.

Off we went, running down the trail that I had run so many times before, but have never seen. We passed the log where Mike and I sat after the big race last year. That is the spot where Mike gave me my new collar that he made for me with all of my racing tags on it. I saw the creek that I had heard so often, with its bubbling waters dancing over the rocks. I looked up and saw the eagles that live near our yard. They were so big and majestic, watching over the trails. I wondered if one of them was the one who landed in our yard after I ran into it. Remember, it tried to snatch little Christmas.

The snow was so bright white and gentle on my paws. The sun was brilliant against a very clear blue sky. I looked over my shoulder and saw the team working together effortlessly. I looked at Mike. He was smiling and looking like he was really enjoying himself. What a beautiful Christmas day this was.

The orphanage was a smallish blue building nestled behind some trees. Mike stopped the sled by the front door and a woman came out. She thanked Mike and said the kids would be out soon to see the gifts, the sled, and the dogs. After a few minutes, the kids came out. There were about 10 of them, all different sizes, shapes, and colors. While they were dressed warmly, their clothing was old and in some cases tattered. However, they seemed very happy, laughing and giggling when they came outside and saw us.

Since the yard was fenced in, Mike let us roam around the yard. The kids came over to Mike and he gave each child their gifts. I sat by Mike's side watching all of this amazing stuff. It made me feel good to see the joy and happiness on their faces as they received gifts. I watched as they ripped off the colored paper. There was a surprised expression on each face as the children opened their boxes filled with a toy, some clothing, and a few of Mary's great goodies. I felt so good to be a part of this.

I watched another child help a little girl over to "Santa" Mike. It was apparent that this little girl was not well. I watched as Mike helped her up to his knee. She was a very pretty little girl. I noticed that her eyes did not focus. She was blind! I saw Mike give the little girl her presents and help her open them.

"Honey," Mike said. "Would you like to play with one of my dogs?"

"Can I?" the little girl asked excitedly.

"Sure," Mike replied. "This is my very special friend Rivers. He, like you, cannot see. You can sit by him and pet him."

"Rivers," Mike said, calling my name. "This little girl needs some TLC, buddy. Can you help me with that?" Not a problem, I thought as I looked at Mike. "Good boy," Mike said as he rubbed my head. Then Mike told the little girl, "Rivers will stay by your side. Is that okay, Honey?"

"Oh thank you, Mister Santa Mike," the little girl said as she sat next to me, gently leaning against my side. As she sat with me, she talked to me as if I was her best friend. She rubbed my ears and I licked her face, making her giggle. After a while, the little girl said she was getting tired and cold. I cuddled up to her while I looked around for Mike. I saw him talking to the lady. I started to howl very softly. I got Mike's attention and he came over. By this time, the little girl had fallen asleep, resting her head on my side. I watched as they took her inside. The lady said that the little girl had been very sick lately and all of the excitement of today probably was just too much for her. I really felt sad for the little girl.

I was deep in thought about her, hoping she would be okay when Sandy came over to me with a piece of rope in her mouth. She dropped it as she said. "Rivers, I am going to teach you to play the tugging game." Sandy had told me about this game when I stayed in her yard after my operation. "I have a short piece of rope," Sandy said. "I will put it by your front paw. Pick it up and start pulling on it. I will be on the other end pulling." She added excitedly, "The one who pulls the rope away from the other wins. It will be fun, ready?"

I picked up the rope and started pulling on it. This was fun. I saw Sandy on the other side pulling also. She was pulling and shaking the rope very hard, while making all kinds of play growling sounds. I also pulled and shook the rope, but soon let the rope go as if I had lost my grip. "I won!" She said. "It was a good game. We can play this when we get back home. I will teach Lakota how to play it with you."

"Thanks," I said. I watched her leave to play with one of the kids. It was easy to realize that while she is bossy and sassy, deep down inside, Sandy is a real sweetheart.

It was fun just watching everybody and everything. Soon it was time for us to return to our home. After Mike hooked us up to the sled in our team positions, each of the kids, except the

little blind girl, came over and gave each one of us a big hug. Some kids had tears in their eyes as they told us how this was the best Christmas they ever had. Mike did not have to say it, but I knew we would be back here often to play with them. I realized today, that racing the trails is not as important as sharing what one has with those less fortunate.

We left the orphanage and headed back down the trail to our home. Wow, who would have thought that this bunch of dogs could make Christmas great for some orphan kids? As we were sledding home, I noticed that the trail looked different now. Yes, it was getting near evening chow and the sunset was reflecting off the snow in different colors! No wonder Mike spent time with me looking at the sunset. He described them to me, but this was just totally awesome!

Mary had our evening chow ready for us. In the bottom of each bowl was a big bone. I watched my buddies enjoy their chow and their bones. I knew they were proud of what we gave to those kids today. I was proud also, but I was concerned about that little blind girl. Guess I am lucky compared to her. Yes, we both are blind, but I have a home filled with plenty of love. I hope she finds her forever home soon.

It was getting dark and I looked up in the sky to see all of the bright stars. What did Lakota say? "There is a star in the sky for each one of us dogs." I wondered which one was mine. I was getting very sleepy but I did not want to go to sleep. I knew that if I went to sleep this dream, if it was one, would be over, or if I can see, I would wake up and be blind again. Nevertheless, in either case, I have buried in my heart and mind all that I saw today, especially all the acts of kindness.

Mike came out of the house to give us our goodnight TLC. I always get mine last. "Well buddy," Mike said, "it sure was a beautiful day". After he gave me my tummy and ear rub, he sat down in the snow with me. "I really wish you could have seen the joy and happiness on those kids' faces," he said.

Mike, you would be surprised if I could tell you I did see all the wonderful things that happened today. I felt sad that Mike would never know his wish came true. He would never know how happy this day had made me.

As Mike described the stars and the moon to me, I looked up at his face. His beard looked almost white in the moonlight and I swear I saw a gleam in his eyes. I am lucky to have him as my

human. Yes, that was another thing to be thankful for. I bet the team is also glad that Mike is their musher.

After he finished telling me about the stars, Mike gave me a big hug and told me it was bedtime. I watched him get up and leave the kennel, and walk back to the big house. I hoped I would never stop seeing his face in my mind's eye.

I took one last long look around the kennel, our home, and then went inside my doghouse.

I laid my head down and went to sleep.

"Wake up, Rivers," I heard. "Wake up, Rivers," the voice said again. When I opened my eyes, I saw Aurora.

"Aurora! I did not think I would see you again."

She replied, "Well Rivers, I just wanted to check with you and make sure you are okay. Are you?" She asked.

"Yes," I said, "I am fine. I had a beautiful day. Thank you for making it so."

"Rivers, you did a super nice thing today staying with that little blind girl when you could have been off enjoying the sights and playing with your buddies." Aurora added, "I heard you were a special dog. Mike says you are a true champion. He is so right."

Aurora continued, "I have a gift for you, Rivers. Because of the unselfish act you did today, the memories of what you saw today will never fade, never. They will always be as real as you saw them today." She said, "This is a special gift because memories tend to fade as we get older."

"Thank you," I said, "but can I ask for one more favor? Can something be done for that little blind girl?" I asked.

Aurora answered, "You know Rivers, you really do have a heart of gold. Mike has already asked his friends in high places for the same thing." She added, "I think his, plus your request, may just do the trick. I will let you know. I must go now." Aurora said, "But I know our paths will cross again."

She turned to me as she was leaving and said, "You know Rivers, whoever said, 'Blind dogs see with their hearts' must have had you in mind."

"Well, Rivers, Merry Christmas. Now go back to sleep." As I laid my head down, I knew I would never see again, but I was not sad. I had received many special gifts that I would cherish forever. I fell asleep counting them.

Lakota's Past

Yes, this was what you would call a five star Husky day. There were cool temperatures, fresh snow, warm sun, fresh straw, and our tummies were full of great chow. We had just returned from a short training run and Mike snacked us on fish-cicles. It was such a nice day that we all took a nap on the fresh straw in the yard.

I am not sure how long we napped. I woke up hearing Lakota whimpering and crying. "Do not hit me, I did nothing wrong. Why are you hitting me? Ow, that hurts. Please stop hitting me." I jumped up because I thought someone was in the yard beating on Lakota. However, I heard no one. Lakota was sleep talking!

He kept saying these things over and over. I nudged him and I guess startled him when I said, "Lakota, wake up, you are dreaming. You are safe, your friends are here."

I could feel him trembling as he stood up next to me. "Are you okay, Lakota?" I asked.

"Yes," he whispered. It was just a dream."

"Some dream," I said. "You were talking in your sleep about someone beating on you."

"Do you think any of the guys heard me?" Lakota asked.

"I don't know," I replied. "Why is that important?"

"I do not want them, and especially Christmas, to know about the dream. I have that dream very often," he said.

"Sounds like this dream bothers you a lot," I replied.

"It does and it comes from a time in my life that I really don't want to remember or talk about," Lakota said.

"Maybe you do need to talk about it. Who knows, Lakota," I said, "maybe talking about it would help you to put it to rest, and you can get on with your life."

I heard Lakota sit down next to me. "Rivers," he said, "you are my best friend, but I am very ashamed to tell you what happened to me. I felt I was a disgrace to our Husky heritage."

"You are ashamed for being beaten?" I replied, astonished. "Lakota, you have nothing to be ashamed of. The persons who beat you should be ashamed of what they did to you. You don't have to beat a dog to get the dog to be a good dog." I said, "I guess whoever did that to you was not too smart."

Now Lakota is a thinker and if you do not know him or respect him, you may think he is slow. He really is not. He thinks things out and then acts. In addition, when he acts, he does the right thing.

Soon Lakota started to tell me his story. Lakota is older than I am. He was born in a place where some of the humans are mean and do not train dogs to be good. Instead they hit the dogs to make them do work or obey. Really bad news.

When Lakota was born, he was a very big puppy. His human did not like him because he ate too much. They gave Lakota very little to eat. Lakota was always hungry. Nevertheless, he grew to be a very big and powerful dog.

His human had children who also abused Lakota by always pulling his tail, poking him in his eyes, or teasing him before they fed him. If they gave him any treats, they would put the treats out of his reach so Lakota could not get to them. However, the worst thing was that they would slap Lakota in his face. Now that is bad stuff. You can make a dog deaf or blind by doing that. Slapping a dog in his face confuses the dog. The dog does not know if he is going to receive a great ear rub or be hit. This confusion may cause a dog to bite the hand in order to protect himself. That is not good. Dogs want to love and protect their humans and their kids, not bite them.

Because he was so big, and most of the other dogs were smaller, they never played with him. Some other dogs would make fun of him, call him names, and gang up on him. They said he was chicken, stupid, clumsy or an oaf. So Lakota kept to himself. He had no friends. He was alone and very sad.

Now the human would hook Lakota up to the sled but did not train him how to run with the team. When Lakota did not quickly figure out what he should do, he got beat. The other dogs would make fun of him because he did not know how to be a team dog.

Lakota had the smarts to be a great lead dog, but no one would train him. And you know, if you are beat or made fun of

when you have a hard time doing something, you are not going to want to do it. It was the same with Lakota. Because the humans made fun of him or hit him, Lakota really hated to run. The humans forced Lakota to run, even when his paws were hurt.

One day Lakota had enough of this abuse and ran away. He figured that he would rather die on the trail then continue to live that kind of life. Now that is ironic. Lakota believed that he was a disgrace to his Husky tradition, yet he wanted to die on the trail. The very essence of being a Husky is to live and die on the very trails we love to run on, especially with a musher that we are devoted to. The fact is that Lakota almost did die on the trail. However, before that happened, Lakota was found and eventually met Mike and me.

When Lakota was finished telling me all of this, he was very exhausted and laid down on the fresh straw. I stretched out next to him and put my head on his shoulder, telling him he was very brave to talk about it. He was still trembling.

"You know, Lakota," I said, "did you ever think that maybe your shyness is due to the fact that you were so alone for so long? No need to answer," I said, "just think about it."

I told Lakota that Mike says Lakota pulls back when he tries to pet him. "I wonder if you do that without realizing it because you think you are going to get hit again?"

"Yes, it must be; it makes sense," Lakota said. "I don't mean to do that. It just happens. I know Mike will not hit me or allow anyone to hurt me. I guess Mike gets a little frustrated when I do." Lakota added, "That is when he puts me in that body hug you told me about, Rivers, and I have to admit it feels so good when he gives me all of that attention."

I replied. "It takes awhile to get comfortable with all of the affection, especially when you never had any before."

"Yes," Lakota said. "I really like it when Mike rolls me over and rubs my tummy. I hear him laugh when he scratches that certain spot that makes my leg move."

I told Lakota he did the same to me. We laughed together.

"Lakota," I said, let me ask you a question. "Do you like running now?"

"Yes," he replied, "I really enjoy it, especially since Mike took special care of me so that my paws healed." He continued, "Yes, Mike does take very good care of me. The chow is great and the team members are my friends and respect me. It is so different

from where I was born." Then in a softer voice, he added, "I never believed I would be trained or allowed to run lead."

We relaxed for a while longer. I sensed that Lakota was deep in thought. "Rivers," Lakota asked, "Do you think some human kids are abused like I was?"

"No doubt in my mind," I answered. I knew this to be true. I told Lakota that Mike reads the e-mail we receive from the kids to me. Some of those kids tell us how bad it is at home for them. I bet some of the kids at the orphanage were abused also.

"That is terrible!" Lakota said.

"Yes it is, but it gets worse," I replied. I told him that I had heard that some humans abuse each other. Some of the strong ones abuse the weak ones. I heard that kids sometimes abuse each other where the big ones pick on the smaller ones.

"That is really stupid." Lakota said, "I thought humans were supposed to be smart."

I told Lakota that most are, but the dumb ones just do not get it. They believe that the only way to succeed is to hurt others and force them to do what the stupid ones want them to do.

"Abusers," I said, "make you think you are the dumb one, like they did to you, Lakota." I asked, "Didn't they make you feel dumb because you were so big and did not know how to run? Didn't they make you feel that you were at fault, and that you were the problem? Didn't they make you feel like you were a disgrace to the point where you wanted to die?"

I could sense the anger in Lakota's voice when he said, "Yes, to all of those, Rivers."

"So Lakota," I asked, "who are you angry with?" Remember that Lakota is a thinker and I knew he was thinking about his anger.

"Me," he said. "I should have been smarter."

"Smarter about what?" I asked. Lakota had no answer. I told him that he was wrong for thinking that. He should not be angry with himself, but instead should be angry with the ones who hurt him. "You did not ask to be beat, or to be made fun of, or forced to be alone," I said. "Actually, anger just adds to the problem. You really need to focus your energy on repairing the damage done and not allow it to stop you from enjoying your life." I paused before saying, "I guess talking about it helps you deal with it in a positive way."

"You know, Rivers, you make a lot of sense. How did you get so smart?" Lakota asked.

"I'm not that smart," I replied, "Blind dogs just see things differently."

Hello Sunny

When Mike told us we would be having a visitor for a few months, we were not surprised. We often have dog guests who need special attention. Some are recuperating from medical problems, while others just need some hands-on individualized training and TLC.

We enjoy having these visitors to our kennel, because we believe in sharing our good fortune, our experiences, and our knowledge with others. We work together as a team to make our visitor feel welcome, enjoy their stay with us, and learn a lot. That is the important thing.

Therefore, we were eagerly waiting for the arrival of our new guest. All we knew was that she was a lady dog who had some medical problems and needed sled dog training.

We were all in our yard. Lakota was standing next to me. He was describing how Ugly and Christmas were playing their chasing game. Lakota also mentioned that Brownie and Nitro were using a piece of rope to play the tugging game that Sandy taught us. I know Doc was standing with us just laughing as Brownie was trying to pull the rope from Nitro. As you know, Nitro is the biggest and strongest dog on our team and no one can beat him at the tugging game. However, sometimes Nitro lets us win so that we will play it again with him.

Doc was laughing and telling me that Nitro let the rope go as Brownie was pulling it very hard. Brownie just flopped across the yard, laughing. As Nitro went over to Brownie to make sure he was okay, we heard Mike's truck enter the driveway. We knew he had our visitor with him.

I heard the guys move closer to the gate and Lakota walked with me. He was telling me that Christmas was scampering all around. She was very excited.

I heard the gate open and I was surprised to hear the guys gasp. What is wrong, I thought. Lakota told me that our visitor was one of the most beautiful dogs he had ever seen. Lakota said that she looked at each one of us and just smiled the most radiant smile he had ever seen. He said she had the kind of smile that just made you want to be her friend.

As I heard Mike lead her into our yard, Christmas was the first to talk to her. "Hi," Christmas said, "my name is Christmas and welcome to our home. You sure are very beautiful."

"Hello Christmas, you are very pretty yourself," the lady dog replied. "Your eyes are so blue and beautiful." We all heard Christmas giggle at the compliment.

When I heard this lady dog speak, I could not believe my ears. Her voice was as soft as fresh snow beneath my paws. She had a voice that you would never get tired of listening to. Moreover, while I know she was talking to all of us, her voice had that quality that made you feel that she was talking only to you.

Christmas asked, "What is your name?"

The lady dog answered, "I have a native name that is very hard to pronounce." She continued, "It translates to 'Beautiful dog with the sunshine smile.' So my friends call me Sunny."

"Awesome!" Christmas said. "That is so cool. I am called Christmas because my uncles, all the dogs here, saved me on Christmas Eve." With that, Christmas introduced each one of her uncles to Sunny.

She saved me for last and then said. "This is my Uncle Rivers. He is blind, but he is the one who found me, and saved me from the eagle, and saved the team from the ice and...."

"Christmas," I said softly. "Enough talk, you are embarrassing me, Little One."

"Please let her continue, Rivers," Sunny said. "If I am to be a good lead dog, I need to learn all the good things that you and the other guys did. Besides," she continued, "my Doctor Jim says many nice things about you and your teammates."

Before I could answer, Doc said, "Sunny, you must be very tired from your trip. May we show you to your doghouse?" He added, "Would you like some water and biscuits?"

"That would be very kind of you," Sunny replied softly. "Maybe after that, we could all relax and talk. I really want to hear all about each of you."

"Me too?" Christmas asked. "Yes, Christmas, you too." Sunny

chuckled. "You know, I am not too much older than you are. I am only two and a half years old."

"Awesome!" Christmas said. "I am just over a year old. You could be like my big sister. I have an Aunt Sandy, but she is very old and…"

It was Lakota who said, "Christmas, Aunt Sandy is not that old. Be respectful, young lady."

"Yes Uncle Lakota," Christmas said meekly. I smiled inside as I wondered if Christmas would be luckier to have six older brothers instead of her six uncles.

Lakota told me that Doc led Sunny over to her doghouse, which was between Christmas' doghouse and mine. I smiled as I pictured it in my mind, Christmas just bending Sunny's ear, asking questions and so on. I cannot really blame Christmas for being excited. She does not get much chance to talk to lady dogs her own age. Sandy is twelve years old, so I do not believe they have too many things in common. Moreover, having six very protective uncles really does not help Christmas with coping with lady dog issues. I chuckled. I hoped Sunny would get some rest.

Evening chow was just great and after it, we all gathered in the yard to talk and share experiences. Since Sunny was new to our home, Brownie asked her to tell us about herself. While I could not see her, I knew exactly where she was by listening to her beautiful voice. I just sat down and enjoyed listening to her.

Sunny's story is very sad. She is Doctor Jim's dog. Doctor Jim is the eye vet who made me pain free and takes good care of all of us. As Christmas would say, he is just awesome!

Sunny was very sick and her owners did not want her because she was a burden. They were ready to send her across the Rainbow Bridge, but Doctor Jim saved her. He raised Sunny and nursed her back to health. It was a long process and Sunny may never fully recover. It seems that every time Sunny made progress, another medical obstacle developed, which she struggled to overcome. As I said, no one knows if she will ever be 100 percent healthy. Nevertheless, Doctor Jim asked Mike to see if Sunny could learn to enjoy her Husky heritage and run the trails.

As I listened to her, I was inspired by Sunny's courage. It is the strong silent type of courage. It shows in her determination to overcome these challenges and never give up. As she told us what she had gone through, it became very apparent that Sunny met her challenges head-on and never felt sorry for herself, even

when her health failed her. It was very clear that Sunny loved life to its fullest and made the most of every second.

The more I listened to her, the more I admired her. If any dog needed a chance to succeed, it was Sunny and I bet the guys were thinking the same thing. We would do everything we could to help her.

As Mike said, it is not the ribbons around your neck, or medals you win, or even the trophies you get that make you a champion. It is what is inside of you. As we listened to Sunny, it was amazing that she had gone through so much yet still had the desire to live up to her Husky heritage. My instincts told me Sunny has the stuff to be a true champion.

While I could not see their facial expressions, I sensed that every dog in our yard would watch over Sunny and help her to do her best. Sunny may never realize it, but she was now "family" with seven friends who would look after her while she stayed with us.

After Sunny finished her story, there was not a sound in the yard except for the gentle breezes blowing through the trees, and that of Christmas crying.

"Why are you crying, Christmas?" Sunny asked.

"Because you had a very hard life and it hurts to know that you lived with all of that bad stuff." Christmas said.

"No Christmas, please do not feel sorry for me," Sunny said. "I actually consider myself blessed." She explained, "Doctor Jim has been a very loving companion and I have friends like you and your Uncles Doc, Nitro, Brownie, Ugly, Lakota and Rivers." Sunny continued, "I can feel the warmth and understanding from all of you and I know that I am very welcome here." She added, "Not too many dogs or people have that. I know you will take good care of me, just like your Mike takes good care of all of you."

Christmas stopped crying and said, "I am glad you came and I bet we will become great friends. My uncles take good care of me, and I know that they will take good care of you too." You could hear the pride in her voice.

Christmas told Sunny about her uncles. "My Uncle Brownie is the fastest dog on our team and the first to defend his friends."

She continued. "Uncle Doc is the smartest and the gentlest. He is a great lead dog and taught us to be good leaders also."

"My Uncle Nitro is the biggest and bravest dog on our team and lets no harm come to any of us."

"My Uncle Ugly is not ugly at all. As you can see, he is very handsome and loves to tell jokes. He will make you laugh when you are sad," Christmas added.

"My Uncle Lakota is very shy, but very, very smart. He is a thinker. Uncle Lakota is a very gentle dog and a great listener. He watches over me and reminds me to be respectful, not only of my elders, but especially of myself."

"My Uncle Rivers is my hero. He saved my life more than once. He saved our team from the ice floats. My Uncle Rivers is blind, but that has never stopped him racing the trails or caring for his teammates."

"When I grow up," Christmas said, "I hope I am like all of my uncles." I was embarrassed and I bet the other guys were also, but I know we were very proud of our little pup. She is becoming quite a lady dog.

"And I bet your Uncles are very proud of you also, Christmas," Sunny said. "But you know what? It is getting late and you know we lady dogs need our rest so that we can look great in the morning."

I know Christmas smiled as she said, "That is so cool. You want to come over to my house and girl talk for a while?"

"Sure, but only for a short while, I am kind of tired," Sunny said, as I heard them walk off towards Christmas' doghouse.

"Ladies." It was Lakota. "Now get some rest, we have work to do tomorrow."

"Yes Uncle Lakota," Both Sunny and Christmas said chuckling.

I knew Lakota was laughing to himself when Nitro said, "Geez Lakota, ease up. This is not boot camp. Let the ladies have some fun. Life is just too short not to have a good time. Besides," Nitro added, "it sounds like Sunny deserves some good times."

"Yeah, Nitro, you are right." Lakota said, "Did you hear the joke about the...."

"Wait a minute, Lakota." It was Ugly. "I am the joke teller around here."

We all started to laugh and went to our doghouses to get some rest.

I was dreaming of leading my team across the finish line when I heard Sunny's beautiful voice saying, "Rivers, wake up, I need to talk to you." What a dream this is, I thought. I am leading my team to victory and Sunny is speaking to me at the same time. It cannot get much better than that.

"Rivers, please wake up, I must talk to you." Again the voice,

however this time I realized this was no dream. The urgency in Sunny's voice woke me right up.

"What is the matter, Sunny?" I asked.

"Can we talk, Rivers?" She asked.

"Of course Sunny, something bothering you?" I asked.

"Yes Rivers, I am scared," she said

"Scared?" I said, leaping out of my doghouse. "Something in the yard?" I asked. "No, no Rivers," she said. "I am scared of tomorrow."

"Tomorrow?" I asked. "What could you possible be scared of?" We both started to walk over to the far corner of the yard so that our voices would not wake the rest of the team. I could tell from her voice that something was troubling Sunny and it would be best to give her some privacy to talk about it.

As we walked, she told me that she had never run in a team before. She was afraid that she would fail, and the guys and Christmas, or Mike or her beloved Doctor Jim would think badly of her.

"Why are you telling me all of this?" I asked her.

"Because you have faced so many challenges in your life and you overcame them. You would know the answer," she said.

I told her that I have no single answer. I face each day as it comes and then deal with its challenges. If I succeed, great. If I fail, so what? I know that I gave it my best shot, and that is all that counts in life.

I also told her that Mike and the team would not think badly of me if I failed. Mike especially. He would just scoop me up, give me a big body hug, and tell me I did great, even if I failed. He would know, as well as my teammates, that I tried and did the best I could. As I said, that is really all that really counts in life.

"But my Doctor Jim wants me to run the trails like you guys and live up to my Husky heritage." She added, "I do not know if I can do that."

"I know your Doctor Jim very well and I will tell you that he just wants you to be happy. Furthermore," I said, "Doctor Jim would be proud of you whether you became the best lead dog in the world, or never ran a race and just curled up in his lap." I continued. "Doctor Jim is giving you a chance to find your destiny. I can assure you that whether your destiny is to be great lead dog or a house dog, Doctor Jim won't care." I added, "He only wants you to be happy. Doctor Jim is very much like Mike;

he will like you no matter what you are. Unfortunately, some humans don't feel that way," I said. "But we are lucky. Mike and Doctor Jim do."

"Rivers," she asked, "will you be my friend?"

"I am your friend." I replied.

"No Rivers," she said. "I want you to be my good friend, my special friend."

I told her I would always be there for her, and I would always be her friend. As I spoke those words to her, I realized that I was becoming very fond of this lady dog. I wanted to protect her from all of the uncertainty she was dealing with, yet I knew she had to experience it herself so she would find her true happiness and destiny.

This was very confusing for a simple trail running dog like me. I was thinking too much. I asked Sunny if she felt better. She said she did and we walked back to her doghouse. I told her not too worry. Things always happen for the best and just to believe in herself. She would do fine.

"You are so courageous, Rivers." She said as we reached her doghouse.

"No," I said. "You are the courageous one. Your life spirit could have given up when you were sick so often. It did not and I know it will not give up on you now. You will be a success at whatever you do. Now get some rest. I know we will have a fun day tomorrow."

"Thank you Rivers, my special bud," she said

"Goodnight Sunny."

Sunny On the Trails

I got up before my teammates and went to the corner of the yard where I know the morning sun will shine on me. Mike tells me that I am looking east towards the sunrise. Sometimes he stands by my side and tells me what he sees. I can picture it all in my mind, as he talks to me and rubs my ears. It is so nice and comforting to be there and feel the warmth of the early morning sun. It makes me feel thankful for all the things given to me.

I heard her footsteps in the fresh snow behind me, but I did not turn around. "Mornin' Sunny, how are you?" I asked.

"How did you know it was me, Rivers?" She asked.

"I heard your footsteps in the snow," I answered.

She said nothing as she sat down beside me. After a moment of two, she asked me what I was doing. I told her I was looking at the sunrise. "But you can't see," she said, "you are blind!'

"True," I replied, "but I can see it in my mind."

"Can you see me, in your mind?" She asked. I told her yes I could. "What do I look like to you, in your mind?" She asked this in a very soft, almost cautious manner. However, before I could answer, we heard the sound of Mike hitting the food bucket with the big spoon and singing, "Hey you sleepy heads, get your fannies out of bed. Chow time!" There is nothing like Mike singing in the morning to get your heart pumping and your legs moving. If the food were not great, Mike would be one lonely critter after singing his morning wake up song!

As we ambled over to the chow, Sunny said, "You didn't answer my question Rivers. What do I look like in your mind's eye?"

I chuckled as I said jokingly, "Well, that is for me to know and for you to figure out."

"Rivers you are so frustrating," she sighed.

"Yes I know but that is what friends are for, right?" I said laughingly. "You better get over to your food bowl and eat that great chow before Sandy gets out here from the house. She likes cleaning up," I added.

I heard Mike scoop out my chow and put it into my bowl. As I stuck my head in it to eat, I could hear my buddies eating and enjoying their kibble.

"Hey Lakota." It was Ugly with his morning joke. "Did you hear the one about…"? I missed the rest of it as an airplane flew overhead. I could tell from the sound that it was Doctor Jim's. I bet he was on his way up north to help the village dogs. Sunny told us that she often went with Doctor Jim on these trips.

After chow, we played in the yard for a while and then Mike came out to harness us up. "Okay gang, this is what we are going to do," He said. "We will make two runs today. The first one will be a short run with only five dogs. Rivers and Lakota will be in the wheel position. Christmas and Doc will be the leaders and Sunny will run as a solo team dog. This way, Sunny can get used to running with the team. We will not be going very far, a few miles or so and it will be a nice gentle pace so that we do not tire Sunny out. She is recuperating and we do not want her to get hurt."

Mike continued, "When we return and get the team watered, we will take another longer run with only six dogs. Brownie and Ugly will be the leaders. Doc and Nitro will be in swing with Rivers and Lakota in the wheel. During the return trip, I will swap Lakota and Rivers in as leaders."

Many people think Mike is a little crazy for talking to us this way. I guess they do not realize that we understand him. By letting us know what he wants us to do, we can do our best for him. I heard that humans have a problem communicating with each other. I have always wondered why.

"You can run lead, Rivers?" It was Sunny.

"Yes I can, but we cannot go too fast when I do and I only run lead in an emergency or on a fun run," was my reply.

"But you can't see!" She exclaimed.

"Yes, I know. You keep reminding me of that." I said a little too curtly.

"I am sorry Rivers, you just amaze me." Sunny said.

"I am sorry that I was short with you," I said. "When I lost my

sight, my hearing, sense of smell and sense of presence, or radar as Mike calls it, intensified. Also, I have my teammates. With them, I have five and sometimes six pairs of eyes."

I heard Mike pull the sled out of the shed and set up the lines. I know that he uses two snow hooks, one in the rear, and one in the front. Mike uses two hooks until he gets the lead dogs harnessed up and snapped into their positions. After the lead dogs are in position, Mike tells them to sit and they do. Then he harnesses the rest of the dogs in their positions with the wheel dogs harnessed last. Once Mike finishes, he pulls the front snow hook and double-checks all of our lines and snaps. After he gets on the runners, Mike pulls the rear snow hook, tells us to stand up, and then says, "Okay team. Get ready. Go!"

I heard Lakota tell Sunny what was happening. Doc was the first one into position. Mike told Doc to sit as he slipped Doc's harness over his head. Once the harness passed Doc's head, Mike told Doc to stand up. Mike then told Doc, "Paw up." I know that when Mike touched Doc's paw, Doc would lift it so Mike could place it through the harness opening for his front legs. I heard "Paw down." and knew Mike would start working with Doc's other paw.

After Doc was in harness, Mike snapped the lines to Doc's harness and collar. Mike then told Doc to sit. He did the same to each of us and saved Sunny for last.

We all told Sunny to listen to Mike and let him get the harness on her. She did. We asked her if the harness was too tight and she said it fit perfectly. She said that Mike gave her a tummy rub, patted her head, and told her she was a good dog.

"Well how do I look guys?" Sunny asked.

I heard Lakota just mumble, "Lady dogs, always worrying about how they look!" and I said she looked great.

"Rivers how would you know that?" She demanded. I heard the guys laugh as Christmas surprised us all with, "Sunny, blind dogs see things differently than we do." You could tell Christmas was very serious by the tone in her voice.

"Where did she get that?" Lakota asked.

"I have no idea," I replied

After Mike secured Sunny into her harness Doc said, "Now Sunny, we are not going to go very fast, so you can just take it nice and easy. You can move to either the right side of the centerline or the left; whichever is more comfortable for

you. Just let Rivers know if you will be running in front of him." Doc continued. "Do not worry about falling or tripping over the lines. The trail is very nice and there should be no holes. Christmas and I will keep the lines taut so they will not get under your feet. Just find your pace and enjoy the run. There is nothing to worry about. Believe me it will come naturally to you." Doc finished with "Does that sound okay to you, Sunny?"

"I am very excited about this," Sunny said. "I know I can do a good job. Thanks for being so kind and patient."

I knew she was very scared, but she was a gutsy lady dog and would do her best. I knew the rest of the team was watching and cheered her on. "Look at that lady dog, I bet she is lead dog material!" That was Brownie.

Ugly added, "You go, girl."

Then Nitro said, "Sunny, show them what a champion looks like." And if that were not enough, all of us started with a "Go Sunny go" chant.

Above the chant we could hear Sandy's' voice saying, "Hey Sunny, show these guys what a classy lady dog can do!"

Christmas told me that there was a big broad smile on Sunny's face. She was really enjoying the encouragement.

I heard Mike get on the runners, pull the rear snow hook, and said, "Okay team. Get ready. Go!"

Lakota and I leaned into our harnesses and got the sled moving. Doc and Christmas pulled the lines tight as I heard our footsteps in the snow. Soon we were gliding down the trail.

Lakota told me that Sunny was in front of him and she was doing okay. She actually was pulling and doing her part. He said she looked very strong and very sure-footed. You would never guess that this was her first time running with a sled dog team.

Lakota said that every time Mike gave a "Haw" or "Gee" command, Sunny would watch Doc to see what he would do. Yes, experienced team dogs watch their leaders. Soon she knew that if Mike said, "Haw," we would go to the left, or if he said "Gee," we would go to the right. If Mike said "Straight on," we would go straight.

Sunny was learning very fast. Doc and Christmas kept asking her how she was doing, and she told them that she was having a lot of fun. She was really enjoying this.

Since Sunny was not tiring out, Mike stayed on the trail a little

longer than he said he would. That was fine with us. It was a beautiful day for a fun run.

We were just easing around a bend when Mike said "Doc, gee straight." Now that means Mike wants the leaders to make a half right turn, which will take us off the trail. We do this if there is another team coming up from behind that wants to pass us, or if we meet another team on the trail. Common trail courtesy is for each team to give the other a lot of room to pass.

However, I could not hear this team moving. I heard Mike say, "Stop. Sit," which means Mikes wants us to stop and sit down. We did that and I heard Mike plant the rear snow hook and get off the runners, while talking softly. Lakota told me that Mike was talking into the little box that Mike called a cell phone.

Something did not feel right. Lakota told me that there was another 6-dog team parked on the other side of the trail, but there was no musher. Mike walked over to the dogs, but they were nervous and cowering.

I heard a voice talking from behind this team. "What are you doing around my dogs"?

I heard Mike reply, "Are you the musher of this team?"

"Yeah, so what?" was the reply.

Mike said, "Just checking to see if you need any help."

"Nope," the voice said, "you can just mind your business and move on."

"Actually, what you are doing here is my business." Mike said. "You are on my property. Moreover, I do not allow people who do not ask my permission to be on it. It is all posted land. Now pack it up and move it out." Mike continued "Oh, by the way the snare traps you are putting out are illegal, and I don't want them on my property."

I heard the musher's voice move closer to Mike and say, "You seem to know a lot, maybe too much for your own good." The voice sounded very menacing.

"You are right," Mike said, his voice not flinching, "I do know a lot, especially about that helicopter you are hearing overhead. It is a state trooper chopper, the one I called when I saw you trespassing and setting up illegal traps. I would guess that all of those pelts you have in that sled are illegal also."

It was very quiet except for the chopper coming closer to us. "One more thing," Mike said, "beating your dogs is also illegal." I heard Mike walk over to one of the dogs on the other team.

"This dog's name is Smokey Joe. I know this dog, I can see where you have beat him."

Lakota told me it was Smokey Joe, and he did not look like the dog we knew. He was cowering, dirty, and looked like he had been beat up a lot.

"Smokey, this is Rivers. Is that you?" I asked.

"Rivers," the dog replied, "yes it is me Smokey Joe. Be careful," he said, "this musher is a very bad person."

The chopper was directly overhead when the musher pushed Mike down and then jumped on the runners of his sled. The team would have run over Mike, but we told the team not to go. They were confused, but did not move. The musher came around to the front of the team where Smokey Joe was, but Smokey Joe jumped the musher. That gave Mike a chance to get up and hold the musher until the trooper chopper landed. Lakota told me that the musher kicked Smokey Joe in the head and Smokey went down, just before the troopers grabbed the musher.

Lakota said that Smokey was not moving and Mike was kneeling next to him. Smokey's head was in Mike's lap and he was gently stroking Smokey's head. Doc said that Smokey opened his eyes. He looked at us and said that he was very sorry for being mean to us the last time we ran together. He said he was stupid for running away. He wished he had raced with us to Nome and honored his Husky heritage. Smokey looked up at Mike, licked his hand, and closed his eyes. Smokey was gone.

Lakota told me that Mike took his knife out of his pocket and cut Smokey Joe out of his harness. The troopers walked up to Mike and he told the troopers that he was going to take Smokey back to our place and give him a decent burial. Mike suggested that one of the troopers drive Smokey's team up to Mike's kennel and he would find homes for the dogs. The pelts and traps were evidence, and Mike told the troopers he would be available to testify against this musher if needed.

Christmas' voice sounded confused and sad as she told me how Mike gently lifted Smokey Joe up off the ground, placed him in our sled basket, and covered him with a blanket. Outside of Mike's commands, the run home was very quiet and somber.

Sunny was stunned. What had started as a fun run, turned tragic. She did not know about Smokey Joe. On the run back home, we told her about how he was a bully, picked on Old Rex and me, plus snapped at Christmas and Mike. We told

Sunny that Smokey did not want to run in the big race, and how he planned to get us disqualified from it. We told Sunny that Smokey ran off and joined a wolf pack after he was dropped at a checkpoint for a phony limp. That was the last we saw of him until today.

We were all silent until Lakota said, "Who would have thought that Smokey Joe would live up to his Husky heritage, to live and die on the trails we love to run and race on?" Lakota continued. "Who would have thought that Smokey would protect Mike?"

After we got home, Mike got us out of our harnesses and gave us fresh water. The other guys were ready for their run, but we told them what had happened. We were all in the yard talking, while listening to Mike in his workshop. He was building something. We walked over to the workshop. The door was open. Ugly was standing next to me and told me what he saw. Smokey Joe was still wrapped in the blanket and resting on one part of the worktable. Mike was building a box that was the same size as Smokey Joe. Doc told us that the box is called a coffin. After we die, our spirits cross the Rainbow Bridge, but our bodies stay here. We will not need them at the Bridge since we will be happy, young, and healthy dogs.

Ugly told us that Mike had his back to us and when he turned around, you could tell he was very sad. I guess Mike saw us standing there because he said, "So you guys are feeling sad also? Well, Smokey may have been a bad dog, but in the end, he was a good dog and a hero." Mike added, "We will remember him for the good and not the bad. That is how we should remember anyone who dies"

Ugly told me that Mike put one of our team harnesses on Smokey Joe. Then Mike took off Smokey's old collar and put one of our team collars on him. Ugly said that Mike took a brush and brushed Smokey out and made him look like the champion he had been.

"You are on my team now Smokey," Mike said, as he gently placed Smokey into the box and put the top on it. Brownie said that Mike's face was a little wet and his eyes were red. Yes I thought, Mike was very sad. As we looked at the box, Nitro said that Mike painted Smokey Joe's name on it and underneath his name the word "HERO."

Mike lifted the box up and I heard him carry it out of the workshop. Lakota was next to me and we walked with the rest

of the team to a hill that is located a little ways down the trail. It is not a big hill, but it looks down on the trail.

When we got to the hill, Lakota told me that Mike put the box down and cleared the snow from the ground. Mike began to dig a hole in the ground. The dirt was not frozen as it was on the trail since the sun warms the ground here. I heard where Mike was digging and I started to dig the dirt by his feet. Next thing I knew, we all were digging in the dirt helping Mike dig this grave for Smokey.

When we were done, Mike placed Smokey's coffin into the grave, and covered it with dirt. Mike said that when Spring comes, he would plant some flowers here and put a marker on Smokey's grave. We sat for a few moments and I got a strange, but nice feeling, that Smokey was across the Bridge looking back smiling at us, and happy with what we did for him. I bet he was truly happy for the first time in his life.

The Night After the Day Before

When we returned from where we buried Smokey, we all went to our doghouses to get some rest. After a while, we all came back out to the yard and started to talk about what had happened. This had been a confusing day. What had started out as a fun day turned into a sad day, which made us think about how lucky we were.

"Uncle Rivers." It was Christmas. "I am confused," she said. I asked her what was confusing her.

She was remembering Smokey Joe as a very mean dog who snapped at her when he visited us before the big race. She reminded us that Smokey had picked on Aunt Sandy and Grandpa Rex. She even remembered how Mike wrestled Smokey to the ground in order to protect us from him. He was a big powerful dog. However, when we saw him today, he looked so old and weak. He even protected Mike. Christmas asked whether she should feel sad or angry.

There was silence until Lakota answered her. He said that we should feel sad because Smokey died, but we should feel very happy that he is in a better place now, and that he turned out to be a good dog. Lakota added that it is all right to feel angry, but we should replace that anger with appreciation and happiness that we are in a good home, with a good musher who takes great care of us.

I was amazed at Lakota for what he said. He really knew the score. However, Nitro finally put this issue to rest when he said, "Christmas, our job as dogs is to be good and to protect our musher. Some of us do and some of do not. Smokey chose not to be good, but in the end, he did the right thing. He proved that good would always win over evil."

This was coming from Nitro. Amazing! Nitro stood nose to nose with Smokey Joe when Smokey picked on Grandpa Rex and me. Sometimes words of wisdom come from the least expected mouths.

"Christmas," Sunny said, "you have some very smart Uncles."

"Yes," Christmas said. "And they are very brave and I am proud of all of them."

"And we are proud of you too Christmas." It was Ugly. "But it is time for you to go to bed and get your rest." He added, "We have to make up for lost training time tomorrow."

"Okay, Uncle Ugly, but who is going to tell me my good night story?" Christmas asked. Each night Brownie, Ugly, or Doc tells Christmas a story. So we were surprised when Nitro said, "I will. Let's go."

"You never told me a story before, Uncle Nitro," Christmas said.

"Well," Nitro said, "There is a first time for everything." He started the story. "Let me tell you about the time a moose and ......" His voice trailed off as they went to Christmas' doghouse.

You could tell Brownie was surprised when he said, "Do you guys think it is a good idea for Nitro to tell stories to Christmas?" He added, "I heard some of his stories and they made me blush."

Ugly chimed in with, "Well Brownie, are you going to tell Nitro that he cannot tell Christmas stories?"

"You must be crazy to think I would dare to do that." Brownie chuckled. "I'd be his next story!"

As we laughed, Lakota said, "You know, I bet there is a soft tender side to Nitro that we have never seen, yet Christmas brings it out. I bet he is very careful with the stories he tells her."

Doc said, "He is very protective of her, just as if she was his own pup. But then we all are. Makes you think a bit about how we all were put in the same place at the same time to save her."

"Jeez, Doc," Ugly said, "you make my head hurt with all of this thinking stuff. I'm going to bed."

I heard them all wander off to their doghouses. However, I did not hear Sunny's footsteps. I turned to her and said, "Well you sure had an adventurous day."

"Rivers," she asked, "how did you know I did not go to my doghouse." I told her that I did not hear her footsteps walk away and I heard her breathing. She was standing right next to me. I turned to face her.

She told me she was still shook up over what had happened. I changed the subject and asked her how she liked running with the team. She really perked up. She was very excited and she told me she liked it and hoped we could do more of it. It told her we would, but we needed to turn in. I told her that I bet Mike would start us early tomorrow. I told Sunny that I knew she had done very well. Lakota and Doc were watching her and said that she ran like a natural. "I bet you will be running lead very soon," I said

"And did you watch me also?" she asked with a smile in her voice.

"Well that is for me to know and you to find out." I laughed.

"Oh Rivers, you are so frustrating," Sunny cried.

"Did we have this conversation before?" I continued laughing and said, "Early to bed and early to rise makes us Huskies healthy, hardy and wise." I continued. "It is past my bedtime, Sunny." I walked her to her doghouse, said goodnight, and started to walk back to mine.

"Good night Rivers, pleasant dreams," she said. Yes, it thought to myself, I always seem to have great dreams.

Mud

The next day Mike started to train Sunny in earnest. At first, we did two short runs per day. Sunny would run in all positions: wheel, team, and swing. She ran on the left side or the right. No matter what position she ran she did great.

Sunny ran with each one of us as a running mate. It made no difference which of us Sunny teamed with, she ran as if she had been running with that teammate forever. Lakota and the guys were talking about how Sunny brought out their best when they were on the trails. Sunny, like Christmas, became a regular member of our team. We were all dreading the day she would go back home.

Moreover, we all knew that Christmas would have the worst time when Sunny had to leave. They had become real buddies. Sunny was a positive role model for Christmas and it seemed that Christmas' boundless energy and eagerness to learn motivated Sunny. Many times when an uncle was teasing Christmas, Sunny would be right there also. As I said, Sunny and Christmas were good for each other.

Both lady dogs were fast learners and when teamed together, they functioned as one dog. Christmas had been running in the lead position at one time or another with all of her uncles. Sunny also had run lead with most of us. However, the day that Mike teamed Christmas and Sunny as co-leaders was the day that Sunny really lived up to her Husky heritage.

This was to be our longest trail run with Sunny. Mike had packed extra gear in case this became an overnight trip, so the sled was heavier than usual. Nevertheless, with eight dogs pulling there would not be a problem. This probably would be our last run of the

season since the temperatures were getting warmer and the snow was disappearing on the trails.

Mike harnessed us up and put us in our positions. Christmas and Sunny were the lead dogs, with Doc and Ugly in the swing position. Next came Lakota teamed with me as the team dogs, and Nitro teamed with Brownie to run in the wheel position.

We were waiting for Mike to give us the commands when we heard Christmas say, "Okay team, the trail is probably really messy, so we are not going to go too fast. We will use the first few miles to get our stride and if we get some good trail, we will speed up the pace a bit. If not," Christmas continued, "we will just lope along and have a nice fun run."

"Christmas," It was Ugly. "You sound just like Doc when he gives us his trail overview."

"No she doesn't." It was Doc. "I don't have a puppy dog's voice like Christmas."

We started to chuckle until Christmas said very sternly, "Uncle Doc, I am not a puppy dog any more. I am a lady dog like Sunny and Aunt Sandy, and I am your lead dog on this run."

I turned to Lakota and said, "Our little pup is growing up."

Lakota told me. "Yep, and we all better start realizing that she is not the little puppy we saved on that Christmas Eve awhile back." Deep down inside, we were all proud of her, even Doc. Yes Doc, you taught her well.

I heard Mike get on the runners, pull the rear snow hook, and say, "Okay team. Get ready. Go!"

We leaned into our harnesses and got the sled moving. Sunny and Christmas pulled the lines tight and I heard our footsteps in the snow. Soon we were gliding down the trail. Well at first, we were, but soon our smooth trail turned into a rutted nightmare with ice and little, or no snow.

As we moved on, the trail just got worse. Mike stopped the team and decided to put booties on us for extra protection.

Lakota told me that Mike was limping. "Must be his bad knee acting up again," I said.

Lakota replied, "And you know this nasty trail is not helping that knee either."

We started pulling again, and started down a hill but then stopped when Mike said, "Stop! Mud! That's it, we are turning back." You could hear the frustration and disappointment in Mike's voice

Going home was okay with us. Besides the mud, the temperature was getting warmer. Lakota told me that the trail was very narrow here and it would be very tricky turning the team and sled around.

"Okay gang." It was Mike. "This is what we are going to do." Mike told us that he was going to unpack the sled, then unhitch the team. Next, he would lift the sled on end and turn it around. Once the sled was turned, Mike would pull it to a spot on the trail a few yards back that was wider than where we were. After the sled was repositioned, he would move the team, hitch us up, and then repack the sled. Then we would be on our way back home.

Good plan, until it started to rain. Of course, it would not be one of those nice misty spring rains. Nope, let us talk deluge! As it rained on us, Ugly's jovial voice rang out with, "Hey, where is Sandy? She is a Labrador retriever, a water dog, and they like this kind of wet weather!" Leave it to Ugly to get us to laugh.

"Hey Sunny." It was Brownie. "How are you doing? You still want to be a sled dog?"

Now you would figure that this lady dog, who does not have a lot of trail time, would be a little frazzled by all of this. Not Sunny. Her voice was clear and calm. You could actually hear the excitement in it. "I'm having great time. Nothing like a little spring rain storm to bring out the best in us lady dogs, right Christmas?"

"You betcha, Sunny," Christmas joined in. "Gee Uncle Brownie, your fur sure looks funny in this rain storm! You having a bad fur day?"

We all laughed at that one. "Where did Christmas learn to tell jokes like Ugly does?" I said to Lakota and he said to me, "Where did she learn to talk like Mike? 'You betcha' is one of his phrases."

"It seems like our youngster is growing up very fast," I told Lakota.

"Have you noticed that neither of them has whined or complained about anything during this entire trip?" Lakota said, "Real champion lead dog material."

"I cannot wait till we get some snow and they run lead with us again," I said.

Nitro must have overhead our conversation. He said, "You know with those two as part of our team, we could be some serious competition in eight dog races."

"Hey Nitro." It was Doc. "Can we get out of the mud first, before we think of crossing finish lines?"

"Okay Doc," Nitro replied, "just a thought, maybe something to keep us motivated during the summer time."

Lakota told me that Mike had the sled repositioned and re-packed. Mike moved to the front of the team and grabbed the neckline between Christmas and Sunny. Mike told Sunny and Christmas to go "Haw." He then told us to go "Gee Straight." What this did was to move the front two dogs to the left and move the rest of the team to the right to make room for the turn. It worked fine.

It was still raining as he hitched us up. Mike got on the runners and said, "Okay team. Get ready. Go!" We barely got the sled moving. It kept sinking in the mud.

"This is not going to work," Mike said. I heard him limp to the front of the sled. Lakota told me he knelt in the mud, and held Christmas and Sunny's faces near his and told them that they must lead the team home. Mike told us that he must help us push the sled and he could not steer it.

What a challenge for these lady dogs! Lead the team home in this kind of weather and on this bad trail. An experienced lead dog would have difficulty doing this. Yet, Mike was asking his two most inexperienced leaders to do it.

I heard Mike limp to the back of the sled, but he did not get on the runners. Instead, he stood between the runners, locked up the drag, started to push, and said, "Go!" We all started to pull at the same time and the sled moved. Not fast, but steady.

We were making progress, but we were going uphill. The rain had stopped and it was getting colder. Maybe we would get some frozen tundra to run on. Not the greatest, very bad on the paws, but the sled would slide better.

We crested the hill and the trail started to level out. I could feel the ground get crunchy under my paws. This stuff could really tear up a dog's paw pads. Pulling our sled in the mud, even with Mike's help, was tough work. Actually, it was harder than pulling a fully loaded sled and musher on a snow packed trail. The guys were all commenting how tired they were getting.

Lakota asked Sunny how she was doing. "Fine," she said, but you could hear the tiredness in her voice. This had to be very tough on her. She was not used to pulling sleds as we were. Remember that she was still recuperating and might not have

all of her strength back. Nevertheless, she held her own and did a great job leading us. Christmas was doing fine also. Yep, her uncles were sure proud of her.

"Team, stop," was the command that Mike gave. We stopped and wondered what he wanted us to do. Lakota told me that Mike set the snow hook and started to walk to the front of the team. Lakota said he was still limping, worse than before. I knew we were all concerned about him. Just as I knew we would get him home, I knew he would also do his part to get us there. Yes, we were a team.

The trail was beginning to freeze. It was not as wet as the muddy part we just left down the hill. As Mike took off our dirty wet booties he said, "Okay Team, lets take a break and get those paws of yours aired out a bit." Next, he set out some water bowls for us and gave us nice treats to go with our drinks.

I heard Mike sit on the sled basket and I heard a zipper unzip. Lakota told me that Mike was rolling up the pants leg to get a look at his knee. Lakota told me that it looked somewhat swollen but there was no blood. Well that was a good sign, I thought.

I heard Christmas turn around and asked what Mike was doing. However, before I could answer, I heard Mike say to her, "Hey my Christmas Girl, you look so sad. Are you Okay? Oh, you are worried about my knee. It is all right, my Christmas Girl. You are doing a great job getting us home."

Lakota told me that Mike rolled his pants leg back down and zipped up his overalls. He got up and limped to the front of the team. "You are all doing great. I could not be any more proud of you than I am right now. That was some nasty trail back there and you got us through it." He then limped to Sunny, put his nose to hers and rubbed the side of her face, "You too, sweetheart. You are a true champion. I know you are not 100 percent yet, but you did not give up. Doctor Jim will be very proud of you when I tell him." Mike continued, "You can run with my team anytime you want." We all knew that made Sunny feel ten feet tall.

After Mike finished talking to Sunny, he came to each one of us, told us that we were good guys and gave each one of us his famous ear rubs. You bet we enjoyed the big fuss he made over us. In addition, we knew that Christmas loved the attention he gave her. She had become very devoted to Mike, just as all of her uncles were.

When he finished giving us all of this praise and attention, he dried our paws with a towel he had in the sled bag. Mike then put some ointment on each one of our paws, especially between the toes. He made sure that our paws were okay, no torn pads, stones, or no ice balls. Next, he put fresh booties on our paws to protect them on the icy trail.

We were ready to roll! The frozen ground let the sled glide more easily. Mike stood on the runners, pulled the snow hook, and said, "Okay team. Get ready. Go!" We were going home and Mike was going to ride this time and not limp. We would make sure of that!

We all knew he was feeling better because he started to sing cowboy music on the way home. Now Mike cannot sing worth a hoot, and cowboy music with a New York City accent would certainly keep any wildlife on this trail out of our way, especially with these words:

> "O mother, don't let your babies grow up to be mushers,
> They'll spend every night with their doggies alone in the snow.
> And when they finally get on that trail goin' back home to ya
> It will be a short time before they gonna get ready to roam."

Sunny, not being used to this, started to laugh and then howl in tune as Mike sang. "Hey Sunny, you have a nice voice, mind if I join you?" It was Ugly.

"Why not," she replied, and soon the two were howling with Mike.

Christmas started next to howl next and soon the entire team was howling as we trotted down the trail going home.

The Short Journey to See Ya

After the muddy trail run, it became very apparent that the snow season was over. I heard the geese flying overhead as they returned from their winter vacations. Soon there would be grass growing in the yard and the soft scents of Mary's flowers in the gardens. The warm season is generally a time of relaxation and easy training to keep in shape for the snow season.

It was a nice day. Sunny, Christmas and I were all loafing in the yard. Ugly was telling jokes, while Brownie and Nitro were swapping trail stories. I overheard Lakota and Doc having a very deep discussion about Husky heritage and we all knew that Sandy was waiting for the carrots to grow, so she could dig them out of the veggie garden. Yes, it was a very nice and peaceful day.

I guess I heard the truck first. I recognized it to be Doctor Jim's mobile vet office. I heard Mike tell Mary that Doctor Jim had returned from the villages and would come by soon to pick up Sunny. I guess we all knew that today would come eventually. Sunny would have to go home, but I know we did not think about it too much. Sunny was a part of our team and we would miss her, especially Christmas. The two of them were great friends, especially after the muddy trail run. What a pair of great leaders they proved to be!

Doctor Jim lives down the trail from us, so we would see Sunny when he brought her by to visit. However, he is so busy helping sick animals in the villages that he is gone a lot. Doctor Jim takes Sunny with him on these adventures. She told me she loves to fly with him and give encouragement to the sick animals he treats at the remote locations they visit.

I heard Mike come out of the house to greet Doctor Jim. They talked about all kinds of stuff as they walked over to the yard where we were. Lakota came up next to me and told me that as soon as Sunny saw her Doctor Jim, she went charging over to him, jumped up in his arms, and started to lick his face. She was so happy to see him. We were all glad that she was so happy.

When Doctor Jim put her on the ground, Lakota said that the expression on Sunny's face changed from joy to sadness as she looked around at us, watching her.

"I am so confused," she said. "I am so happy to see my Doctor Jim, but so sad to leave all of you. You have all been so good to me, treating me like your family."

I heard Christmas standing behind me, crying softly. I guess the reality that Sunny would have to go home really hit Christmas hard. I heard all of her uncles move closer to her, offering comfort. Sunny walked over to Christmas and said, "Oh Honey, I am so sorry that I have to go. But you know I must. I live just down the trail from you and I bet that Mike will bring you over to visit. I know that my Doctor Jim will bring me by often. I truly believe that we will run the trails together again, Christmas." Then she said, "I want you to know that you are like a sister to me."

Lakota told me that they nuzzled each other and a slight smile returned to Christmas's face. Then Sunny walked over to me and asked. "Do you know where I am Rivers?"

"Yes," I replied, "you are right in front of me, about 6 inches from my nose."

Then she said very softly, so that only I could her, "You don't know how much confidence you gave me to run these trails with you and our teammates. I was very scared and doubted I could do it. I was afraid to fail, but you made me realize that I could do anything I set my mind on doing. You made me understand and be proud of my true Husky heritage. I am a better dog for it. Thank you, Rivers."

I was barkless, but did manage to say, "Sunny, it was always within you to be a true champion and you are. If you did not have the desire, we would not be standing here barking today." I continued. "Since I know deep down inside that our paths will cross again, I won't say goodbye, but rather 'See ya'."

Sunny said, "In your mind's eye I suppose?"

I answered, as I laughed with her, "And that too." .

"What is happening here Mike?" It was Doctor Jim. "I have never seen dogs act like this. It looks like they are sad and saying their good-byes."

"I think you hit the nail on the head, Doctor Jim," Mike answered. "They have been working together as a team and living together as a family." Mike continued. "I am sure that they developed bonds probably stronger than we give them credit for."

"Interesting," Doctor Jim said. "I have never thought of it that way, maybe you got something there. I would love to spend some time discussing it, but there is a sick poodle at the Jones' place that I need to check on before I go back home."

I heard Doctor Jim snap a leash on Sunny while asking, "Mike, where did Sunny get this new green collar with her name in gold letters from?"

Mike answered. "Well Doctor Jim, it is a gift from the team and me. We also had a harness made for her in our team's colors. We did not think you would mind and we hope that Sunny can run with us when we get some snow on the ground."

Doctor Jim was laughing as he said, "Looks like my girl got adopted and well taken cared of by your team. And from what you were telling me about how well Sunny ran, it would be a crime not to let her run with your team." He added, "Yes, let's count on it! And maybe Christmas can come to my clinic and visit us.

All right Doctor Jim! Sunny joins our team and Christmas can visit her at Doctor Jim's clinic. Super! I know that made us all happy, especially Christmas.

That's What Friends Are For

The warm weather came and with it, the snow vanished. After the snow melts, the trails become too muddy to run. Mike takes us for walks and he spends a lot of time in our yard with us. He plays the tugging game with us. This is a game played with a piece of rope. Mike grabs one end of the rope and one of us dogs will grab the other and we each pull, and the last one to drop the rope wins.

Sometimes Mike will swing us around as we hold on to the rope. Other times he will shake it a lot. It sure is a lot of fun. Normally Nitro, who is the biggest and strongest dog, will go first. However, today Nitro said he wanted to go last. I know he had something planned.

Poor Doc, who is the gentlest dog and the smallest of us, went first. Lakota told me that Doc did not make it past the first good hard pull. Mike went over to Doc and made a big fuss over him. Although he did not win, I know Doc felt good for trying hard and getting all of the praise Mike gave him.

Lakota told me that Mike stood there with the rope in his hand and Christmas walked up to it and grabbed it. She held it good and tight. Christmas pulled the rope. Mike pulled harder and shook the rope, but Christmas would not let go. Christmas pulled and shook the rope, but Mike would not let go. The guys were all standing by me watching Christmas and Mike in the tugging game. Mike would pull harder, and then Christmas would pull harder. Neither would give up, until the rope broke! Lakota told me that Christmas fell backward, saying she won.

Mike ended up sitting on his butt, laughing. Doc told me that Mike got up and walked over to Christmas and just rubbed her a lot, making a big fuss over her. Nope, we were not going to tell

her the rope broke. Let her believe she won. It would not hurt to make her feel good. She had been so down since Sunny left.

Mike got another piece of rope. Ugly said it was his turn. Now Ugly, who is a clown, said he was going to have some fun. He just grabbed the rope and sat down. When Mike pulled the rope, Ugly just sat there and let the rope go. When the rope fell to the ground, Ugly would jump up on his hind paws and do his "Ugly Jig," which always makes us laugh. Mike just grabbed Ugly and gave him a big tummy rub.

Well that left Nitro, Brownie, Lakota, and me. Nitro told us that he was going next. He told us that after he grabbed the rope, all of us should grab it also. When we were pulling very hard, he would give us a signal to let the rope go. Mike would fall backward into the straw pile and then we would all pile on him and wrestle.

Now that sounded like a fun plan. Doc told me that Nitro walked over to the rope. Mike had a good grip on one end and Nitro grabbed the other. Nitro began to pull and so did Mike. Brownie told us they pulled so hard that the rope stretched very tight. That is when we all jumped in and grabbed on. Doc, Ugly, and Christmas joined us. There were seven dogs pulling on the rope that Mike held. We pulled and he pulled. As Mike pulled harder on the rope, Nitro told us to let go and we all did at the same time.

Christmas started to giggle as she told me that Mike fell backwards into the straw pile just as Nitro had said he would. We all ran over to Mike and jumped on him, licking his face and sitting on him. He pushed us away or grabbed one of us and rolled us in the straw. Doc said that Ugly actually jumped on Mike's back trying to do his "Ugly Jig" until Mike shook him off.

The bell rang. Mike has a little box that he can talk into and it rings when someone wants to talk to him. Doc said it was called a cell phone. Once it started to ring, Mike stood up and started to talk.

"What do you mean, Doctor Jim, someone took Sunny out of your yard?" Mike asked. "You saw them head down the trail towards us?" Mike said, "We are on our way."

Sunny stolen! Then I heard her howl. It was a very painful howl.

I turned to the guys and said, "Sunny is in trouble. I heard her. She needs our help. Follow me!" I started to race out the open gate. I heard the guys and Christmas follow me.

"Stop!" It was Mike, but this time we must disobey him. He needed to follow us.

We headed down the trail. I was running as fast as I could. I had never run this fast before, but I had to get to Sunny. She kept howling and I knew exactly where she was from her howls.

Brownie was behind me. He is normally the fastest dog, but this time he could not keep up with me. "Jump, Rivers, a log!" and I jumped as he told me to do.

Sunny,s howls were getting louder, but there was another animal near her, a wolf!

I could hear Brownie's footsteps fading to my rear. I was on my own until the gang caught up.

I found Sunny. "Rivers, I am caught in a snare and I think my leg is broken. The wolf attacked me and I am bleeding," she said.

"What is this? A dog coming to stop me? A blind dog no less," the wolf said. "What a joke."

I needed to buy some time. I was no match for this wolf. "Yes Wolf, a blind dog." I said defiantly, as I got between Sunny and the wolf. "A blind dog with friends." I added, "You better move on while you still can."

Then I heard Brownie. "Hey Wolfie you don't want to deal with a sled dog with attitude, do ya?" Brownie was starting to sound like Mike.

I heard Nitro and Lakota race off the trail next, snarling and barking at the wolf. However, the loudest and nastiest barking came from Christmas as she cleared the trail and got up front with the wolf.

"Mister Wolf," she started, but before she could continue, we heard Mike on the four-wheeler yelling, "Down, down!" We laid down and I heard two shots ring out from Mike's gun. Doc told me Mike missed the wolf, probably on purpose, and the wolf ran off into the woods.

"Sunny," Mike said. "It is okay girl. Let me help you." Lakota was next to me and told me that Mike cut off the snare that was around Sunny's rear leg. Yes, Sunny's leg was broken.

Mike gently laid Sunny down and put his fingers into the bloody fur on her neck. "Puncture wound." Mike said. Lakota told me that Mike took a tube of something out of his pocket and squeezed the contents into the wound. Then Mike took a kerchief out of another pocket and tied it around her neck to help stop the blood flow. He then took two small tree limbs and tied one on each side of Sunny's broken rear leg using the snare wire. This

way, the leg could not move and cause any more damage to the broken bone.

Doc said Sunny did not look well at all. Doc told me that Mike took the cell phone out of his pocket and started talking into it.

"Doctor Jim," Mike said. "I found Sunny. Broken rear leg and a puncture wound on her neck from a wolf." Mike continued. "I have the leg splinted but I don't know if I stopped the bleeding. I got the wound loaded up with antibiotics and covered. I am about 2 miles from my home. "Can you meet us there?"

Brownie told me that the four-wheeler had a little trailer behind it. Mike wrapped Sunny in his coat and gently laid her in the trailer. He then grabbed my collar and told me that I needed to get in the trailer and cuddle up to Sunny to keep her warm. He told Lakota to do the same. I heard Christmas jump in also.

Mike told the rest of the team, "Home" and Lakota told me that they followed us up the trail to the house.

When we got to the yard, Doctor Jim was already there. "Let's use your warming shed," Doctor Jim said as Mike lifted Sunny out of the trailer. I jumped out and Lakota led me into the warming shed with the rest of the team.

"You did a good job with her leg splint, Mike," Doctor Jim said. "We can deal with that later. The neck wound is bad and she has lost a lot of blood." Doc told me that Doctor Jim was talking to Mike as he cleaned and then examined Sunny's neck wound.

Christmas was standing next to me and asked me if Sunny would be okay. I said, "You bet Little One, Doctor Jim is the best." I hope I sounded convincing for both our sakes.

"Mike we need to do a dog to dog blood transfusion," Doctor Jim said.

Mike answered, "We have eight donors here, Doctor Jim."

"It is not that simple," he said. "First it would be very unwise to transfuse blood from 8 different dogs into one injured dog." Doctor Jim explained, "That would greatly increase the chances of a severe, possibly fatal transfusion reaction like a bad penicillin or bee sting allergic reaction in people." Doctor Jim continued, "But there are other reasons not to use a dog as a donor. For example, the donor dog should be at least 44 pounds. That leaves out Doc, Christmas, Ugly and Brownie who weigh less than 44 pounds."

"Dogs should be between 1 and 6. So, that leaves out Sandy since she is 13. He said

"Also the donor dog should be the same blood type. Type 'A' is universal canine donor and Rivers, Nitro and Lakota are all type A. Remember, we did blood work on all of your dogs last year."

Mike asked, "Okay so who should we go with?"

"My first choice would be Nitro since he is the biggest and has the most blood." Doctor Jim answered. "After Nitro, I would use Lakota and Rivers."

Doctor Jim continued. "However, before we do the blood transfusion, I will need to repair the artery that the wolf nicked. That nick is causing the blood loss. If I can get it to stop, then we can go ahead with the blood transfusion."

"We are going to give blood to Sunny." It was Nitro.

"Yeah," Lakota said. "And you are going to be first, Nitro."

"Guys," I said, "I have to be the first to do this."

Lakota asked, "Why be first Rivers, we may all get to donate blood to Sunny."

I replied, "That may be true, but I need to be sure that I do this. It is for Doctor Jim." I went on, "He made me pain free and this would be my way of thanking him, helping to save his beloved Sunny."

"This could be dangerous for you Rivers, you are barely 50 pounds." Nitro said in a very calm voice. He continued, "And Doctor Jim said the bigger the dog the better for these transfusions. Lakota and I have 20 pounds on you."

"I am willing to take that chance," I replied. "Besides, if it were not for Doctor Jim, I would never have been able to enjoy racing or running the trails again. Sometimes I feel that I have been selected to do something special and this may be it. Please guys," I begged. "Let me be first."

I had to do this and the guys knew it had to be me. They agreed and the plan was that every time Doctor Jim or Mike went to pick up Nitro, I would get in the way and Lakota would block them. We hoped they would get the idea that I must be first. Nitro would be second and Lakota third. The other dogs agreed to help by blocking Nitro.

I heard Doctor Jim tell Mike he was ready for Nitro. When Mike went to get Nitro, five dogs blocked Mike. I was in front. "Team, I have to get Nitro." However, the team sat there shielding Nitro. When I heard Mike try again, I jumped up and put my front paws on his chest.

"Okay Rivers, what is going on?"

Come on Mike, you are a smart human. Can't you see that I want to be first and that the team is telling you that by blocking Nitro?

Mike picked me up and said, "Doctor Jim, we are going to use Rivers first." As he put me on the table next to Sunny, I could hear her breathing, very slowly, very softly. I am sure she was resting. If her eyes were open, I am sure she would have said something to me. I was becoming very worried and scared. Did I do the right thing? What if Sunny needs more blood than I can give her?

"He is the smallest of the three, Mike. I have to be careful how much blood I take out of him," Doctor Jim said. "Hmm, he was very calm when I operated on him. He will be Okay." Doctor Jim continued, "That gives us the two bigger dogs in case we need more."

"Yes," Mike said. "I bet they had this plan to let Rivers be first. Makes you wonder sometimes how smart these critters really are."

I felt the needle prick into my front leg where Doctor Jim wanted to take the blood. I heard my teammates move closer to the table. "Are you Okay Uncle Rivers?" It was Christmas.

"I am fine Little One, don't worry."

"Rivers, is that you?" It was Sunny.

"Yes, it is me," I replied. "Don't talk. You need to rest and let the blood transfusion work," I said.

"Rivers," she said. "Will you tell me how you see me in your mind's eye?"

I answered, "Only if you get better and we run the trails again."

She asked, "You promise?"

I answered. "Do you promise to get better?"

"Yes," she said as she drifted off to sleep.

I heard Doctor Jim say, "All done, Rivers, you did a good job." I never felt him take the needle out of my leg. Mike picked me up and laid me down in the big pile of straw that we have in the warming shed. I heard Christmas come over and sit next to me.

"Well Mike," Doctor Jim said. "I think we did it, but we will not know for sure for another 12 hours or so. Do you mind if I keep Sunny here for the night?"

"I was going to recommend that since Nitro and Lakota are here and you might need them," Mike said. "Let me get the team fed and watered." He added, "I am sure they are hungry after this adventure."

I heard Mike command the team back to the yard for chow.

They all left, knowing Sunny needed her rest. I needed mine also and I was just about to doze off when I heard her silky soft voice say, "Thank you, Rivers."

I heard Mike and Doctor Jim come in and out of warming shed several times. I just rested there in the soft straw listening to Sunny's breathing. However, nature does call and I headed to the yard. I wandered over to a far corner and softly howled my prayers for Sunny into the quiet of the night.

I felt a dog sit besides me. I was puzzled since I did not hear any footsteps. There was no dog scent either. "Who are you?" I asked.

"Now Rivers, I feel hurt that you did not recognize me," a familiar voice chuckled.

"Aurora!" I said excitedly, "Aurora Gooddog! What are you doing here?"

"She answered, "I am here for you, Rivers. You did some very brave things today, even risked your own life for your friend," She said. "Racing down that trail as fast as you could, and not being able to see. Facing that wolf, knowing you had no chance against it. After defending your friend, you gave her some of your blood. That is a lot to do in just one day. You made me proud that I am your Guardian Angel Dog."

I replied, "My friend needed help and that is all that matters. I know she is destined to fulfill her Husky destiny." I paused, and then said. "What do you mean, Guardian Angel Dog?"

Aurora answered, "Humans have Guardian Angels. Dogs have Guardian Angel Dogs. Most adult humans forget about their Guardian Angels when they grow older. Most dogs do not know they have a Guardian Angel Dog. We kind of watch over you."

"Do Sunny and my teammates have Guardian Angel Dogs? I asked.

"Yes and no," she answered. "I won't tell you about your teammates except for Christmas, she does have one."

"And Sunny?" I asked. "Nope, not yet."

"Why?" I asked.

"We just have not gotten around to it yet. Besides there is a shortage of Guardian Angel Dogs, right now." She continued, "See, Rivers, Guardian Angel Dogs are dogs who have crossed the Bridge and have shown that they care for others. Once they do that, some are given the job of Guardian Angel Dog.

"Will you be Sunny's Guardian Angel Dog?' I asked.

"I am too busy. I have a bunch of dogs to take care of," Aurora replied.

"Okay," I said. "Let her have my spot on your list of dogs to watch over."

There was silence. "Rivers, why would you do that?" Aurora asked.

"Because she has been through so much that she needs and deserves a Guardian Angel Dog. I have done a lot. And I bet you were there to smooth trails for me as I ran them so I would not fall or trip and let my teammates down." I pleaded, "Now it is her turn."

"Rivers, you are a true champion to think of someone else like that. Okay, tell you what I will do. I will sign on as Sunny's Guardian Angel Dog and make time for her and you also." Aurora continued, "You can never tell her or Christmas about this. They have to believe on their own. Agreed?" she said as she put her paw on me.

I replied. "Agreed. Thank you Aurora. Will Sunny get better? I asked

"I don't have any idea about that nor any power to help," she answered. "The power to heal comes from within you. Sunny has a strong desire to live and since you seem to know her pretty well, then you know the answer to your own question," she said.

Aurora continued. "Well it has been fun chatting with you, Rivers, but I have work to do. Take care." With that, she was gone.

I walked back to the warming shed. I lay down next to Sunny. I must have awoken her because she said, "Hi Rivers, good night," and she went back to sleep.

Mike woke me up and said, "Mornin' buddy, you must be hungry. Here is some chow for you."

"Yes Rivers, it is chow time." I jumped right up when Sunny said that. "You okay?" I asked.

"A little weak and this thing on my leg itches, but other than that, I feel pretty good. Now," Sunny continued with a stern tone in her voice, "you promised me that if I got well you would tell me what I looked liked in your mind's eye, Rivers."

"Are you sure I said that?" I joked. "You were pretty out of it last night and after I gave you some of my super high test, grade

'A' Alaskan Husky blood, I got a little tired. I do not remember saying anything like that."

"Mister Rivers!" she demanded. "What do I look like in your mind's eye?"

"Okay Sunny, don't get your fur up. You look like a pretty lady dog with a thing on your rear leg!"

"Rivers, you are so frustrating," she shrieked.

"Yes, I know," I said as I laughed, "That's what friends are for."

Randy

Mike and I took a walk on a trail that I had never walked on before. This trail was on some kind of hard stuff that Mike called sidewalk. There were many people walking on the sidewalk and Mike told me that there were some benches where people could sit down and rest. Mike said we were in the town near where we live. Mike told me that a town is a place where the stores are located, where he can buy things like food and sled dog harnesses. This is a little confusing to me. Is the town the place where Mike hunts for our food?

It was very noisy and busy, but I was not scared. Sure, I could not see all the things around me, but Mike was with me and he is a good leader. He would talk to me and describe all of the things that were around us. When Mike describes things to me, I can see them in my mind's eye.

Anyway, as we were walking, Mike told me that we were passing a bench and there was a young boy sitting on it with a book in his hands. I heard a young boy say, "Hey Mister, can you help me?"

We stopped and I turned toward the voice. Mike asked, "Are you talking to me, son?"

"Yes sir," said the young boy. "I need help reading this book. I don't read so well."

Mike sat down on the bench next to the boy and I sat between Mike's legs. He asked the boy for the book. "Why son," Mike said, "this is the Bible." I could hear Mike thumb through the pages. "And it looks like this version is a very old version and has not been updated to make it easier to read and understand." Mike continued, "This book would be hard for many people

without reading challenges to understand, son. So don't be too hard on yourself because you have trouble reading it."

The boy sounded relieved, but he was still tense when he answered Mike. "But I still have to read it", the boy said softly. "My teacher tells me that I have to read a lot more and this is the only book I own."

This was becoming very interesting. Here was a young boy and it was apparent that he had some difficulties. Mike asked him where he lived and what school he went to.

Mike's questions just opened the floodgates for this young boy to talk. Randy was his name and his parents had hurt him a long time ago. Then he went to several temporary homes, but they were always too poor to buy him anything. He had missed a lot of school since he was bounced among so many homes. He said he was 10 or 12 years of age. He was not sure, never had a birthday, he said. I really felt sad for this young boy. He indeed had a rough life and had so little. I wished there were something I could do for him. Maybe Mike would know how we could help him.

"Do you mind if I pet your dog, Mister?" Randy asked.

"My name is Mike, Randy, and my dog's name is Rivers," Mike answered. "Yes, son, you may pet him."

As Randy petted me, Mike told Randy all about me.

"Mister Mike, you mean Rivers is blind but still ran the big race to Nome? How could he do that?" Randy asked.

"It takes courage to do that, and that courage comes from within you," Mike answered. "If you believe in yourself, you will accomplish amazing things." Mike continued. "You can overcome all kinds of challenges as long as you want to succeed."

I guess we sat there for the better part of the afternoon. Randy did a lot of talking. What he said made me more thankful for the many things I have. It also made me more appreciative of the simple things like a warm bed, good friends, and hot chow.

Now I was thinking of what I could do for this young boy, when Mike said, "Randy, it is getting late. Would you mind if Rivers and I walk you home? We can talk some more on the way."

While Mike and I lived in the country, we do have neighbors around us, and it turned out that Randy lived down the trail from us.

When we got to Randy's home, I heard Mike talking with Randy's foster parents. They agreed that Randy could visit us at

our home. That would be just great. Mike gave Randy directions to our home.

The next day, we were in the yard when Randy came by. I had told the team about Randy, so Christmas, Lakota, and the rest of the team made a big fuss over him. He was giggling and laughing as we jumped all over him.

Mike was with us in the yard. He was sitting on a bench, and I could hear him laughing as Randy played with the team. Even Sandy was in the yard making a big fuss over this young boy. Mike said, "Hi Randy, how you doing? Come over here, I have something for you". Lakota told me that Mike had a book in his hand.

When Randy sat next to Mike, Mike gave him the book, Lakota told me.

"Wow, my own Bible!" Randy said very excitedly. As he turned the pages, he started to read the words out of it. Mike helped him with the words that he stumbled over. He asked Mike many questions about what he read. Mike answered each of them. Lakota told me that the entire team, and even Sandy and Christmas were sitting around Mike and Randy listening to them talk.

"You know what, Mister Mike?" Randy said. "I think I want to be a writer."

"Why?" Mike asked.

"So that I can write books for kids that have a hard time reading like I do. What do you think, Mister Mike? Do you think I can do it?"

"Yep," Mike said, "And I bet you would be great at it too. Just remember that as long as you believe in yourself and want to succeed, you will accomplish amazing things in your life."

I heard Mike stand up and say, "Okay team. Trail time." As we started to scamper around the yard, Randy asked Mike what was trail time. We all stopped playing around when we heard Randy ask this question. He did not know what trail time was! Lakota told me that Ugly and Brownie went over to Randy and nuzzled his hand. I guess we were feeling bad. If Randy did not know what trail time meant, then he never had experienced the fun of sledding on the trails.

"Randy," it was Mike. "Trail time is the way I tell the team that we are taking the sled out for a run on the trails."

"Oh," Randy said sadly. "I guess it is time for me to go then." Hold on here, I thought. Why does Randy have to go? I think

Mike must have read my mind because he asked Randy why he thought he had to go.

"Well Mister Mike," Randy said, "I don't have any winter clothing or boots to do that. I figured you would want to be alone with your dogs and didn't want me around."

"I think you thought wrong, my friend," Mike gently said to Randy. "Come with me." Lakota told me that they headed for the warming shed where Mike keeps our sled and our equipment.

We all followed them. Lakota told me that Mike gave Randy two boxes. "What are these Mister Mike?" Randy asked.

"Well," Mike answered. "I think they are two boxes that need a young man like you to open and find out what is inside of them." Now Mike had me wondering. What was in the boxes?

Lakota told me that when Randy opened the big flat box, he gasped. Lakota told me that Randy held up a green and black storm suit, just like the one Mike used when he took us on the trails. Christmas said that one time she curled up in Mike's storm suit when she was a small pup. It was so soft and warm. "Yeah, I remember that." It was Nitro. "You snored almost as loud as Mike does."

"Uncle Nitro!" Christmas shrieked. We all chuckled at the way Nitro was teasing Christmas. Yep, our little Christmas was growing up and her Uncles had the gray hair to prove it!

"I wonder what is in the other box," Doc said. Lakota told me that Randy opened the other box and pulled out a pair of snow boots, socks, gloves, and a musher's cap.

"These boots and socks will keep your toes warm, Randy. They are good to 100 below zero." Mike said. "Now, how about getting that gear on while I get mine on, and let's harness this team up for a ride!"

"Thank you Mister Mike, I don't know what to say."

Mike answered, "You said enough son. You are part of our team now, so shake a stick and get dressed."

I heard paw steps and Lakota told me that Brownie and Ugly ran over to Randy and started to nuzzle him and lick his face. Yes, Randy was now officially part of our team!

When they were dressed, Mike pulled the sled out of the warming shed and Randy had our harnesses. Lakota told me that Mike laid out the gang and tug lines. Next he showed Randy how to harness us up. Lakota told me that Mike let Randy harness up Ugly and Brownie.

Next, it was my turn. "Paw up, Rivers," Randy said and I lifted my paw so that he could put the harness around it. He learned quickly and was very good. You could tell he was comfortable working with dogs. His voice told me that he enjoyed working with us. "Okay Randy," Mike said. "We will have Christmas and Nitro as our lead dogs with Doc running in a solo swing position. Brownie and Ugly will be in the team dog position with Rivers and Lakota in the wheel." Mike continued. "I will explain all the positions to you as we travel down the trail. It will make more sense then."

Lakota told me that Mike helped Randy into the sled basket and then Mike got on the runners. "Okay Team, Ready!" I heard the snow hook pulled from the snow. "Set!" I leaned into my harness ready to start. "Go!" We were off.

The trail was nice and smooth. Fresh snow on our paws made the running easy. It was a nice run. Christmas and Nitro were having fun leading. Ugly was telling jokes. Lakota was describing the trail to me. Mike was telling Randy about the commands, what each dog position does, and how he steers the sled.

I am not too sure how long or how far we ran. It was a nice gentle pace, more like a restful trot. I heard Mike say, "Team stop" and we did. Then Mike said, "Team sit!" and we sat.

Mike told Randy that it was time to head back because it was getting late. However, before we headed back, Mike said he wanted to change some dogs around. He moved Doc into solo lead and moved Christmas and Nitro into the swing position. I heard Mike whisper something into Doc's ear as he moved the team around. Lakota told me both Mike and Doc were grinning

After we turned in the right direction to go home, Mike told Randy to get out of the sled basket and get on the runners. Lakota told me that Mike then pulled the snow hook and got into the basket.

"Okay Randy, take us home." Mike said.

"But. But." Randy said.

"Randy," Mike said, "believe in yourself, and tell the team to take us home."

"Okay Team," Randy said. "Get set. Go"! As we headed back home, I figured out what Mike had whispered in Doc's ear: Take it nice and easy and let us build up Randy's confidence.

For a kid that had never been on a sled before, Randy did pretty darn good. He leaned into the turns just as if he had been doing it forever.

Soon we were home and Randy said, "Team stop." You could tell he really enjoyed what he was doing and had a new level of confidence. His voice told me that.

Mike showed Randy how to get us out of our harnesses, check our paws for sores, stow the sled and our gear, plus give us fresh water. Mike told Randy that it would be a smart idea for him to leave his mushing gear here in the warming shed, so that he would always have it ready for trail time.

"Mister Mike, thank you," Randy said.

"My pleasure," Mike replied.

Randy asked, "Mister Mike, will you show me the rest of the things I have to know to be a good musher?"

"I would love to Randy, but I am not a good musher. I just get by," Mike said. "But what I will do is get my friends Stan Smith and GB Jones to teach you. Stan and GB ran the big race to Nome twice." Mike added, "If you are going to learn something, learn it from the best and Stan and GB are among the best."

"You really think they would help me?" Randy asked.

"If you are willing to learn and do the work, I am sure they would be happy to coach you." Mike said. "Think about it and let me know." Mike continued, "Of course we will have to ask your foster parents, but I will do that."

Okay, Mister Mike, I will think about it and let you know," Randy said.

"Now you need to do me a favor," Mike said. "You said you wanted to be a writer, remember? Well, I want you to write a story of what you did today. Can you do that?"

"I think so, Mister Mike," Randy said.

"Nope," Mike said. "Not I think so."

Randy picked up the hint and said. "I can do that and I will have it for you very soon."

"Those are the words of a true champion," Mike said. "It is getting late and we better get you home. How about we put Ugly and Brownie on some leashes and they can walk with us?"

As the four of them walked down the drive to the trail that leads to Randy's home, we all gathered in the yard to talk. "Awesome!" It was Christmas. "Randy was a very happy camper today. Sure makes me feel good that we could share the fun of trail running with him."

Yes, I thought, it is just awesome how much joy a random act of kindness may do.

Christmas' Aunt Sandy

$\mathbf{N}$ow after the puppies came...
Oh, I forgot to tell you about the puppies. Christmas had them.
Yep, she had three of the most beautiful puppies we had ever
seen. Well, that the gang had ever seen. Me, well that is a different story. However, the guys were great at describing them to
me. I have a good picture in my mind of what they all look like.
Mary named them Tundra and Stormy (they are twins), and Sky.
Tundra is the biggest of the three. Tundra is mostly black with
some brown markings. Her ears do not flop over. Stormy looks
very similar to Tundra, but Stormy's ears do flop over and she is
a bit smaller. Both look similar to Nitro, big and powerful. Sky
looks like her mother Christmas, and has her mother's piercing
light blue eyes.

We do not know who the father is. It is not one of us. Mary decided
that Christmas should have at least one litter. So a while back, Mary
took Christmas and.... Well the rest is history.

Of course, when we found out, we were very happy for Christmas. However, Sandy was really excited. Sandy never had puppies. She spent the better part of her day taking care of Christmas. Sandy would scold us if we played too hard with Christmas. She actually got Mike to let her stay in the yard at night
with us. Now that is very strange for a housedog! Good thing it
was springtime. Sandy would have a problem sleeping outside
in the winter, when it is very cold. Besides having a thin coat,
Sandy is sort of old.

When the puppies arrived, Sandy was right there, taking
great care of Christmas. Nitro, who is very good friends with
Sandy, said that Sandy acted as if the puppies were her own.
Wow, these pups had two moms and six grand uncles. Did I

say that? Grand Uncles! I could feel the gray hair growing each day.

A few days after the pups were born, Mike brought home a wheeled sled or training cart. Lakota said that it looked a little like a regular sled but had wheels on it. Mike told us it was made by his good friend Mike Fisher, who lives in Oregon and builds these sleds for dog mushing on the sand dunes down there. So now we can go sledding when there is no snow. I know that mushers use these things for keeping their teams in shape during the summer months. We do not run hard or fast because of the heat, but we can sure get a good workout with the wheeled sled.

Young Randy was with Mike and he sounded very excited that we could go sledding in the summer. Randy had been reading us his stories about dogs and mushing. We were very impressed. They were very good. Brownie and Ugly kidded us that Randy's best stories are about them. Sure glad you guys were objective!

Anyway, I was getting excited. Okay, come on, let us try this thing out. Mike and Randy headed to the warming shed to get our gear. As Mike set the lines out, Randy harnessed us up. I heard Christmas say she wanted to go.

"No, child," it was Sandy. "You need to get your rest and take care of your babies."

Doc added, "Sandy is right, Little One, you need to rest and take care of your pups, so that they will be ready to run with our team soon."

"You are right, Uncle Doc, I am a little tired," Christmas answered. "Don't have too much fun without me." Now was that a play for sympathy or what?

Mike told us that we would head on down the road to Doctor Jim's place, about a half a mile or so, and then head back home.

The wheeled sled was very easy to pull and before we realized it, we were at Doctor Jim's homestead. He and Sunny were out making house calls so Mike checked his house to make sure it was okay. We turned around in a big lot and headed back. We were just entering our driveway when I smelled it. Wolf! "Team. Stop. Down!" were Mike's commands. He wanted us to stop and lie down. "Bam, Bam." I heard Mike's gun and then heard him jump off the sled and run to the kennel. "Randy, take care of the team," Mike shouted.

Lakota told me that there was a big wolf in the kennel and Sandy was down. Christmas was in her house with her puppies. Mike was kneeling by Sandy.

I heard Mike talk very softly to her. He called Doctor Jim on the cell phone. After Randy took us off the gang line, we gathered around Sandy. Doc told me that Sandy was in bad shape, with many bite wounds. Nitro said the wolf was dead, but it looked like he had been in one nasty fight.

"Sandy?" Brownie asked.

"Yes, Aunt Sandy." Christmas was crying. "That wolf dug a hole near the back corner and crawled in while we were napping," Christmas said. "Aunt Sandy heard it, and I was ready to fight it but she told me to stay in my doghouse and protect my babies. I watched from the door. It was a real bad fight." Christmas added, "No matter how nasty the wolf got, Aunt Sandy would not let him near my doghouse. I wanted to come out to help her, but she kept telling me to stay in my doghouse."

Christmas told us that they were still fighting when Mike shot the wolf.

"What can I do, Mister Mike?" It was Randy.

Mike had a hard time answering. "Let's get her into the warming shed. I do not think she is going to make it." His voice was trembling when he said, "I don't want her dying here in the dirt. She is my housedog. I want to get her into a shed."

Lakota told me that Mike gently picked Sandy up and carried her to the warming shed. He placed her on blanket and let her rest on the straw.

"Gang." It was Sandy. "Are the babies safe?"

Nitro answered, "Yes, the wolf is dead." He added, "Mike shot it. You did good, Sandy." You could tell that Nitro was choking back his tears.

I heard Christmas burst into the shed, crying. "Aunt Sandy..."

"Hush child," Sandy said very lovingly. "It is time for me to go. Please listen very carefully to me. While Mike has a bond with the guys and especially Rivers, you child, will have a special bond with him as I do." Sandy continued. "As these guys take care of him as their musher, you must take care of Mike as your human. You promise me to do that?" Sandy asked.

"Yes Aunt Sandy, I will take great care of Mike," Christmas answered, with tears in her voice.

79

Then Sandy said, "Nitro, we never got to play the tugging game. I wonder who would have won if we did."

Nitro answered, "You would have. I am no match for a class act like you." I thought I heard Sandy chuckle.

"Rivers."

"Yes Sandy," I answered.

"I am glad you came into Mike's life. You are very good for him. So are the rest of you," she said weakly to the rest of the team

Lakota told me that Sandy raised her head up a bit, looked right into Mike's face, and said, "You saved me many years ago. You took good care of me and gave me plenty of love and affection. You were a good companion to me. You made me happy. Thank you." She nuzzled Mike's hand, laid her head in his lap, and then she was gone.

I heard Mike sob "Oh, Sandy Girl, my Sandy Girl." Doc said Mike just sat next to her stoking her head, crying softly.

I heard the truck pull into the driveway, then footsteps running to the shed. Lakota told me that Doctor Jim and Sunny came into the warming shed.

"I am so sorry Mike, I could not get here any faster." Doctor Jim said.

"I know," Mike said. "She was badly hurt when I got here. I do not think we could have saved her. She must have tangled with that wolf out there. My Sandy Girl got between the wolf and Christmas' puppies. Looks like Sandy put up quite a fight."

Mike continued, "Doctor Jim, would you mind taking care of that wolf out there and driving Randy home? I have some things I need to do right now."

Doctor Jim answered. "Sure, Mike. Come on Randy," Doctor Jim said, "let's leave Mike alone."

I heard Nitro run out to the yard and start to bark and growl. I ran out with the team and Lakota told me Nitro was barking and tearing into the dead wolf. "If I had only been here." Nitro repeated, "If I had only been here." He was beyond anger. He was in full rage and none of us was going to stop him. I heard Doctor Jim say "Nitro, stop." However, Nitro just ignored him and continued to tear into the wolf. Nitro was beyond listening.

"Uncle Nitro, please stop." It was Christmas. Brownie told me that Nitro looked at her and the fury was still raging his eyes.

"Go away Little One," Nitro demanded.

"No Uncle Nitro, not unless you come with me." Christmas replied.

"Go away, I said," Nitro repeated in a very menacing tone. Christmas walked up to Nitro and stood between him and the wolf. She stood face to face with him. Doc said, this meant that Nitro was head and shoulders over her.

"What you are doing, Uncle Nitro, scares me," she said. "The wolf is dead. It was not meant for you to be here to fight it. It was meant for Sandy to protect me and my babies."

Lakota told me that Nitro just looked at Christmas and moved around her to get to the wolf. Christmas again moved into Nitro's way. Again nose-to-nose, Christmas said, "Uncle Nitro, what you are doing is not right." She then asked Nitro to stop and walk with her.

This was getting very tense. We all wondered what Nitro would do. "Nitro, sit. Team, sit." It was Mike. Lakota told me that he was in the doorway of the warming shed looking at us. We all sat, including Nitro. I heard Mike walk out of the shed and Lakota told me that he was walking towards Nitro.

Lakota told me that when Mike was near Nitro, he knelt by Nitro and hugged him. Lakota told me that Christmas walked back to where we were. I heard her sit next to me. She was trembling.

As Mike hugged Nitro, Lakota told me that Doctor Jim and Randy removed the wolf and carried it to Doctor Jim's vehicle and left. Mike started to talk very softly to Nitro. I do not think anyone could hear him except me, since my hearing is so keen.

"Nitro," Mike said very gently, "I know if you had been here that wolf would have never dug into the kennel." Lakota told me Mike gently rubbed Nitro's head and ears. "I know you would sacrifice your life to protect anyone on this team. You are a true hero and champion, but venting your anger on that dead wolf proves and achieves nothing." Lakota told me that Mike sat down next to Nitro, who rested his head in Mike's lap. "Nitro, do not blame yourself for this," Mike said. "That is the same wolf that attacked Sunny when she was caught in that snare. Remember? I could have shot it then, but I did not. I allowed it to live." Mike continued very sullenly, "If I had shot it, it would not have dug into the kennel and…" His voice trailed off. Lakota told me that Nitro lifted his head and started to lick Mike's face as Mike put a big hug on him.

Lakota told me that they sat there for a few minutes. Then Mike got up and went to his workshop and we heard him start to build something. Nitro came back over to where we were and said to Christmas, "You are a very brave and wise dog, Little One. I am very sorry for scaring you." He paused, and then added, "I am also very proud of you."

Christmas answered, "That's okay Uncle Nitro, I understand." Then she said, "I have to go and feed my babies. You okay, Uncle Nitro?" She asked.

"Yes, now I am," Nitro replied. "Thank you."

As Christmas walked to her doghouse to feed her pups, Ugly asked Nitro what Mike had said that made him calm down. He told us.

"You mean that was the same wolf that hurt Sunny?" Brownie asked.

Nitro answered, "From what Mike said, it was."

"Gee." It was Ugly. "I bet Mike feels terrible. If he had shot the wolf, then Sandy would still be alive."

"Yes," I said. "Mike probably does feel terrible. Mike made the decision to spare the wolf's life. I wonder if Mike still believes that was a good decision."

"We will never know," Doc answered. "At the time Mike made that decision it was a good one. There is no need to kill or destroy something unless you really have to, and at that time, the wolf was not a threat. Most wolves will not come near a kennel or bother a Husky since we are related. However, this wolf was unusual. Let's not judge all wolves by the actions of this bad one." Doc said, "I am very sure that, if Mike knew that wolf would dig into the kennel, he would have shot it back then. But none of us knows what will happen tomorrow, do we?"

The noise in the workshop stopped and I heard Mike walk out of the workshop and Doc told me Mike headed toward the warming shed. Lakota told me he had a medium size box in his hands. I bet it was a coffin for Sandy.

We followed Mike to the warming shed and Lakota described what was happening. The box was a nice wooden box with Sandy's name on it. Mike fetched Sandy's blanket from the house and placed it in the box.

Then Mike brushed Sandy's coat and made it shine. He placed Sandy in the box, wrapping her in her blanket. Mike put in

Sandy's house toys and I heard him drop in a few biscuits in there. "So you do not get hungry on your trip across the Bridge, my Sandy Girl."

Lakota told me that Mike just stood there looking down at Sandy resting in the coffin. It was very quiet. I heard Christmas walk in and sit down. Soon Mike placed the top on the coffin. He carried it outside and placed it in the basket area of the wheeled sled. Lakota told me that the lines were still hooked to the wheeled sled. I just noticed that I still had my harness on. I guess in all of the excitement and sorrow Randy forgot to take them off us.

Lakota told me that Mike put a harness on Christmas. "Christmas, you will be the lead dog." Mike then hooked the rest of us up. Mike said, "Sandy always liked riding in the basket so let's give her one last ride, Team." Then Mike said, "Okay, look sharp, let's go." We trotted down the trail, made a turn, and came back. We circled the house and Mike halted us by a flower garden on the sunny hill across from the big house. Lakota told me that you could not see this garden from the kennel. We had never been here before.

Lakota told me that the garden had many pretty flowers in it and a nice path that went by all around the garden beds. Behind the garden beds were some trees that blocked the wind and added shade from the afternoon sun. There was a bench or two. While I could not see it, I felt the peacefulness and beauty of this garden. It felt like a very special place.

We stopped by a garden bed that did not have any flowers in it. Doc told us this was what the humans call a gravesite. After Mike dug the grave, and placed Sandy's coffin in it, he said, "Sandy, you gave your life to save another. You may never have run a race, but you were true champion, a real hero. See ya, my Sandy Girl." Mike was still for a moment or two.

Then Lakota told me that Mike turned to the rest of us in the team and said. "This is my special garden where all of you, my special dogs, will rest when it is time for you to cross over the Bridge."

Mike then got on the runners of the wheeled sled and said, "Christmas, lead us home." Lakota told me that Christmas turned to Mike, barked once, and led us back to our yard.

Blindness of the Snow

Rivers' Christmas Story, 2002

Christmas time was fast approaching and I was reflecting on the past Christmases that I had spent with Mike, Mary, and the team here at our home. I remembered the first one where we saved a puppy on Christmas Eve and Mike named her Christmas. She is now a part of our family. Then last year, I was able to see for one day. It was Mike's wish. That is when I met the little blind girl at the orphanage.

We have gone back to the orphanage often this past year. My buddies played with the kids, but the little blind girl just sat by me, talking. She treated me like her best friend. I guess the other kids just do not play with her. I can understand that. For many years, I was alone also.

While many of the kids in the orphanage have left, new ones arrived to fill their beds. Mike explained to me that the kids who left were adopted. They went to new homes with new parents. Sounds like what Mike did for me several years ago. However, Mike told me that he was very sad because the little blind girl may never find a forever home. People want well kids, not those with problems.

That made me sad also. Wait a minute, I know. I will give my Christmas wish up for the little blind girl and hope that a nice family will adopt her. That would be awesome if that happened. Oh yes, the little blind girl would be very happy and so would Mike. What did he tell me, "It is better to give than to receive." So that is it: I will give the little blind girl my Christmas wish.

Whenever I really need something, my Guardian Angel Dog, Aurora Gooddog, shows up. Today was no exception.

"Hi Rivers," she said. "What is this I hear about your giving your Christmas wish to the little blind girl at the orphanage?" I

told her what I wanted. While I cannot see Aurora, I know what she looks like since I can see her in my mind's eye. Aurora sounded like she was not looking too happy.

"Rivers, I cannot give you your wish," she said. "I can only help dogs and only those that I am a Guardian Angel Dog for, like you. I am sorry."

Wow, was I disappointed. "There must be a way for that little blind girl to get a new home for Christmas," I said.

"Rivers, it would take a miracle to get that little girl into a home by Christmas. Christmas is only a few days away. Rivers, Guardian Angel Dogs do have limits. I am very sorry, Rivers. I cannot do this for you. Maybe you should wish for something else."

"No!" I said, "I have everything I want, I just want that little blind girl to be happy."

"Tell you what," Aurora said. "Let me do come checking on that and get back to you. No promises. I do not know when I will find the time. You know this is my busy season. However, I will try. I have to go."

I said goodbye to Aurora and she was gone. Well, if I cannot get my wish for the little blind girl, then the best I can do is give her some extra TLC when I see her next.

When we got up the next morning, Mike told us it was Christmas Eve and we were going to deliver our gifts to the orphanage today. Mike told us we were going a day early since we have many guests visiting us on Christmas Day and it would be impossible to get away then.

After morning chow, Mike got the sled out and harnessed us up. Lakota told me that Mike had on his red Santa suit and packages wrapped in colorful paper filled our sled. I hoped there was something special for the little blind girl in the sled. She really deserved it.

I could not believe how fast the time went. It seemed like a very short time from when we left our home until we returned. "Santa Mike" gave out all of the presents. My buddies played with the kids and the little blind girl sat with me and talked and talked. She was hoping she would find a nice home with nice people to live with. She said she had been an orphan for as long as she could remember. Hmmm, was it me, or was the hug she gave me longer and tighter? I licked her face and it was wet with salty tears. Please do not cry little girl. There is a family out there for you. I know there is. I felt so sad for her.

86

Christmas morning came and Mike came out to feed us and spend some time with us before the guests arrived. He gave each of us a new tennis ball. Of all the things that Mike gave to us, he learned very quickly that tennis balls were our favorites. The team loves it when Mike plays catch and fetch with them. Mike taught me also and I can find a tennis ball on the second bounce. That is unless Lakota or Christmas catches it on the first bounce and holds it. Yes, we play a lot together.

The snow started to fall very gently, but I knew that it would turn into a bigger storm shortly. There would be no sled time today, especially with guests coming to the house. That is, if they make it through the snow. So, you can imagine how surprised we were when Mike came out of the warming shed with our sled, lines, and harnesses.

"Okay team," Mike said. "We are going to the orphanage. The little blind girl is missing and the orphanage staff has asked us to help find her. We had better find her quickly. This may turn into one nasty storm."

Oh no, I thought, not the little blind girl. The guys and I had talked about her after we came back from the orphanage. We all hoped she would be all right.

Mike harnessed us up and put us in our team positions. Doc and Christmas were the lead dogs while Brownie and I were in the swing position. Ugly ran as a solo team dog with Lakota and Nitro in the wheel.

"I guess you are wondering why I teamed you up this way," Mike said. "I put Lakota in the wheel with Nitro because you guys are my most powerful dogs. If this storm drops a lot of snow on the trail, I need you two powerhouses back there to get us moving."

Mike added, "I put Rivers up front with Brownie in the swing position. We may have to rely very heavily on Rivers' keen hearing and sense of smell to find this little girl, especially if this storm turns into a blizzard."

"And Ugly, you are in the middle running solo until I find another dog or two that we will need for the race."

"Race!" Nitro exclaimed. "No one told me about a race."

"Me neither," Lakota added. In fact, this was the first any of us had heard about our running any race. I guess we were all lost in our thoughts as Mike finished harnessing us. I heard him pull the front snow hook and double-check all of our lines and snaps.

After he got on the runners, Mike pulled the rear snow hook, told us to line up and said, "Okay team. Get ready. Go!"

We raced down the trail toward the orphanage. I was thinking how scared the little blind girl must be. I know the feeling. It happened to me when I first went blind and became lost in the kennel.

"Whoa, Team stop." Mike's command roused me from my thoughts as we stopped in front of the orphanage. Brownie told me there was a lady in the doorway. I heard her talk to Mike, telling him that the little girl's name was Caitlyn and that she had been gone for about an hour. She became separated from the kids she was playing with and they returned to the orphanage without Caitlyn.

Mike asked the lady what Caitlyn was wearing. A lightweight winter jacket and regular clothes, the lady told Mike. She also told Mike that she called the State Troopers but they could not send up their helicopter due to the storm. The storm! Yes, I sensed it was getting closer. The last thing the lady said was that State Troopers were busy with a very nasty vehicle accident on the highway and that it would be hours before they could send anyone to help.

Brownie told me the snow was falling faster. I turned my head skyward and felt the snowfall on my face. Yes, a very nasty storm!

Mike asked the lady to get an article of Caitlyn's clothing. A hat or scarf that Caitlyn wore recently would do just fine, Mike said. By the time the lady returned, Mike had switched our team positions. I was now the lead dog with Doc. Nitro and Lakota were still in the wheel. Christmas and Brownie were in the swing position and Ugly again ran as the solo team dog.

Lakota told me that the lady gave Mike a stuffed toy. The lady told us that this was Caitlyn's teddy bear and that she slept with it. "That will work," Mike said. "Now may I talk to the kids who saw Caitlyn last?"

After Mike talked with the kids and knew where they had last seen Caitlyn, I heard him walk over to me and kneel down in front of me. I smelled the teddy bear Mike was holding. He put his hands on both sides of my face and put his face close to mine. "Rivers," Mike said. "We need to find the little blind girl that sat with you when we visited here. You are her only chance. This storm is getting worse and the team will not be able see her. You can smell her and you can hear her." As he spoke, he held the teddy bear in front of me and I could smell Caitlyn's scent on it. Yes, I remembered her scent.

We started down a new trail that we had never been on before. Mike was driving the team very slowly. Every once in a while, he would call out, "Caitlyn, Caitlyn, where are you?" Mike stopped the sled and we all strained to hear her call back. Nothing.

Mile after mile we traveled, but all we heard was the noise of the wind getting louder. The temperature was dropping and the snow was building up on the trail. Doc said that the heavy snow would cover any tracks Caitlyn might have left on the trail.

"It may even cover the trail totally," Ugly said.

"Are you saying we need to go back, Ugly, without the little girl?" It was Nitro.

"No, no Nitro", Ugly replied. "All I meant was that if this snow gets any deeper, I won't be able to do my Ugly jig when we do find her!" We all chuckled. Yep, leave it to Ugly to get us to laugh in a bad situation.

Mike stopped the team to put booties on us. What is that? I thought I heard something. It was very hard to tell with all this wind noise. Wait, I heard it again. "Uncle Rivers, your ears are twitching. Do you hear something?" Christmas asked me.

"Rivey, do you hear something?" It was Mike. Yes, I heard something. I also heard Mike unzip the sled bag and listened to him walk back to me. I heard him snap on a leash, while un-hooking my neck and tug lines.

"Okay Rivey, let's go," Mike said. I started to walk slowly down the trail. I suddenly cut to my left, off the trail. I heard Mike following me. I would stop occasionally to listen and sniff the air. Yes, I did hear something, but I was not sure what it was. Could it be a moose or a bear? I could be leading Mike into some big trouble. I was getting scared. I heard a voice speak to me. It was Aurora. "I am here for you Rivers, you are doing fine. Find Caitlyn, you can do it. Trust and believe in yourself."

I stopped again and, yes, the scent. It was coming from over there. I started to bark as I walked faster to where the scent was coming from. I stopped. Caitlyn had to be here. Her scent was so strong. "Rivers, there is nothing here, just mounds of snow," Mike said.

She had to be here. I sniffed the ground. Yes, she was here. Then I heard it, a whimpering. I started to dig gently in the snow and suddenly felt the warmth of her face on my paw.

"Rivers, you found her!" Mike said. I heard him kneel down

beside me and he dug with me in the snow. There was a lot of snow covering Caitlyn. She was alive. She was shivering. She was very cold and she was crying.

"Who are you?" Caitlyn asked.

"Hi Caitlyn, it is 'Santa Mike' and Rivers. We are here to take you home," Mike said.

"Home to the orphanage?" she asked. "No, I do not want to go back there. Nobody wants me because I am blind. I will never be with a family. Nobody wants a blind kid. Just let me stay here, in the snow."

"I can't do that, Caitlyn." I heard Mike unzip his parka and put it around her. I moved closer to Caitlyn to cuddle with her. She put her arms around me and continued to cry, even harder than before.

"Caitlyn," Mike said. "Lets go to my home for a day or so and talk this over. Maybe what you need is a few days away from the orphanage to get your thinking straight. What do you say?"

"Does Rivers live with you?" Caitlyn asked.

"Yep, he sure does," Mike answered. "Say, I could use some help since I have a race coming up. Maybe you could help me out?"

"What could I do? I am blind," Caitlyn replied.

"Yep, you sure are and so is that dog you are sitting next to, and he is the one who found you. Oh, by the way, he is one of my racing dogs." Mike said. "Just think, Caitlyn, if Rivers had given up because he was blind, maybe no one would have found you. Isn't it interesting that a blind dog found you, a blind girl, covered with snow in a blizzard?" Then Mike changed the tone in his voice and asked Caitlyn, "You are not telling me that my blind dog can do more than you can, are you?" Mike asked. "Think about it, Caitlyn."

I heard Mike pick Caitlyn up and start to sing, "Jingle Bells" as he carried her back to the sled. I guess the blizzard affected my hearing because he sounded pretty good and we all know that Mike does not sing worth a hoot. I heard the team howl and bark. They were happy we had found Caitlyn. Nitro told me Mike unzipped the sled bag, got his sleeping bag out and wrapped Caitlyn in it. He then put her in the sled bag and zipped it up so that only her head showed. He put a musher's cap on her head to keep her head warm. I heard her giggle.

Next, I heard Mike walk back to me, and he hooked me into the team as the lead dog. Then Mike said, a lot louder than he really needed to, "Okay Rivers, lead us home."

Now, any of the other dogs could have led us home. Nevertheless, Mike was proving a point to Caitlyn and you can bet your last dog biscuit that I was going to do my part.

We stopped at the orphanage to tell them we had found Caitlyn. After the lady talked to Caitlyn, we were off to our home.

When we got home, Mary met us in the yard and told Mike that the guests that were going to come could not get out of the city due to the storm. Mike told Mary that we had a very special guest who was going to stay with us for a few days.

"Oh?" she said, surprised. "Company?"

"Yep," Mike replied as I heard him unzip the sled bag. "Caitlyn, meet Mary. Mary, this is Caitlyn. She is the little girl from the orphanage I told you about. She was lost in the woods and Rivers and the team found her. I talked to the lady at the orphanage and she said that Caitlyn could visit us for a few days."

"Hi, Caitlyn and welcome to our home." Lakota told me that Mary put a big hug on Caitlyn as she welcomed the little girl to our home. "Now let's get you inside, out of this storm, and find some warm clothing for you. I bet you are hungry. I have a big pot of stew cooking, and some homemade bread for you," Mary said.

I heard Mike say, "As soon as I finish talking care of our canine heroes here, I will be in to join you".

"Now Mike, do not take too long. Caitlyn looks very hungry and she just might eat your portion," Mary said jokingly. We all laughed at that, including Caitlyn.

After Mike took care of us and they ate their chow, Mary and Mike came out to the yard and moved us into the warming shed. This is another Christmas treat. We can loaf in the nice warm straw. Caitlyn was with them and Mike led her to the straw pile and told her that the dogs were going to play in the straw and they would play with her too. Lakota told me that Ugly was doing his "Ugly Jig" while Brownie and Doc were nuzzling next to Caitlyn. I heard her giggle. Lakota told me she had a big smile on her face. Caitlyn was sure a different little girl now than the one we found in the snow today.

I was standing by Mike and Mary. I enjoy listening to them talk about things other than dogs and running the trails. Mike told Mary that he was thinking about adopting Caitlyn and wondered what Mary thought about his idea.

Wow, Mike does not mince his words, does he? Mary said that she had been thinking the same thing since Mike had told her

about Caitlyn after last year's visit. "No kidding!" Mike was excited. "We can do this, you know. We can give her a good life and tutors to get her up to speed in school. I bet I could train some of the team to be her Seeing Eye dogs and...."

"Hold on, Mike," Mary said. "Slow down. We need to know if Caitlyn wants to do that and if the orphanage will let us do it."

"Hmmm," Mike said. "The orphanage is really no problem. They are a private operation and will be glad to place Caitlyn with us since she is probably classified as hard to place. As for Caitlyn, well, let's ask her."

Before Mary could utter a sound, Mike said. "Hey Caitlyn, I have a question for you." I heard Mike walk over to the straw pile where Caitlyn was sitting with my buddies.

Mary grabbed my collar and walked me to the straw pile and whispered, "Rivers, you had better come also. You are a big part of this. You found her and saved her. Now if she is willing, we hope to give Caitlyn a good life filled with plenty of TLC."

As we got near the straw pile Lakota told me that Mike was sitting next to Caitlyn, with his arm around her shoulders. All of my buddies were sitting in a circle around them watching.

"Caitlyn," Mike said, "Mary and I want to know if you would like to live here with us permanently. That means never going back to the orphanage except to get your stuff. Going to school and being a part of our family. What do you say?"

Silence. Not a sound, no person or dog moved. Silence. Come on Caitlyn, I thought, say yes.

I heard Mary sit down next to Caitlyn and I sat directly in front of my little blind friend. Lakota moved next to me.

Lakota told me that Caitlyn turned towards Mike and put her hands on his face and said, "You have a beard, Santa Mike. What color is it?

Mike answered, "Gray and white."

Then Caitlyn said, and I could hear the tears in her voice when she asked "Are you Santa Claus?"

"No honey, I am not. Why do you ask?" Mike replied as he chuckled.

"Because," she cried, "every year at Christmas, I wrote to Santa asking him to give me a forever home and I never got it. This year, I did not write and you are asking me to stay here with you and Mary and your dogs. I thought that you might be Santa giving me my wish."

"No Caitlyn," Mike said, "I am not Santa and these are not just

my dogs, these are my buddies. They are part of our family and we are asking you to join us."

Silence again. However, Mary broke the silence when she said, "Maybe Caitlyn needs some time to think about it, Mike. She has had a rough day."

"No!" Caitlyn said. "Is Rivers here?"

"Yes," Mike answered. "He is sitting right in front of you."

"Is Rivers really blind?" She asked.

"Yes," Mike answered.

"Can he do all of the things that you said he could do?" Caitlyn asked.

"Yes," Caitlyn, I would not lie to you," Mike answered.

I moved closer to Caitlyn, licked the tears on her cheek and put my paw on her leg. She put her arms around me. As she hugged me, I heard her say, "Oh yes, please, I want to stay with all of you!"

Yippee.

Later after everything settled down and I was alone in the yard with my thoughts, I sensed a dog next to me. I knew it was Aurora, my Guardian Angel Dog. "Hi Aurora, thank you for making my Christmas wish come true."

"Rivers," Aurora replied, "I had nothing to do with that. My help stopped after you found Caitlyn in the snow. The magic of the season made your wish come true, Rivers. Good things happen to good dogs. Besides, I told you that Mike has some very good friends in some very high places. Well, I guess he had the same wish as you did."

Aurora continued, "Well Rivers, I would really enjoy spending some time with you, but 'tis the season for me to be busy. So I have to go."

"Can I ask you a question?" I asked.

"Sure," she said, "but make it quick and easy. There is a collie that will give birth to a litter tonight and she is going to need my help delivering those pups."

"My question is this. What do you wish for at Christmas time?"

"Rivers, you think too much. I am in a rush, but the short answer is nothing, since Guardian Angel Dogs need nothing. However, I wish for everything for the dogs that deserve their wishes to come true."

"See Ya."

And she was gone.

A Surprise Visit

I will make no bones about it. I truly miss Sandy. I guess humans call it grief when someone you care for leaves you. Dogs grieve also. However, we would rather remember the good times we had with our buddy, and not pay so much attention to the loss. We know that our buddy has gone to a much better place.

I was doing just that, sitting in my favorite corner of the yard, just after the sun settled down for the night. The guys were resting and they were not paying too much attention to what I was doing.

I guess I was laughing aloud at some of my fond memories of Sandy, when I heard a voice say, "So what is so funny, Rivers?"

Then a second voice said, "Yes, Rivers, what is so funny?

I recognized Aurora's voice and I guess I looked puzzled because the second voice said, "Rivers, you don't remember me?"

"I am sorry," I said, "Your voice does sound familiar, but I just can't place it."

"Gee Aurora," the voice said, "live with some bozos, clean the extra biscuits out of their coops and as soon as you are gone, poof, they forget all about you."

"Sandy!" I said.

"Yes it sure is," Sandy said.

"But, but…" I tried to speak.

"You know Rivers, you sound like a motor boat, going 'but but.'"

I heard both of them laughing. I could not be dreaming, I mean, I was sitting here. It could not be Sandy. She crossed the Bridge after she fought the wolf when she protected Christmas and her puppies. I was confused.

95

"Rivers, Aurora said, remember a while back when I told you we had a shortage of Guardian Angel Dogs?"

"Yes," I replied.

"Do you remember I told you that special dogs are chosen to be Guardian Angel Dogs?" I nodded.

"Well," Aurora said, "Sandy was chosen."

"Sandy, a Guardian Angel Dog?" Yes, I was impressed and very happy for Sandy.

Aurora continued, "Sandy gave up her life to save Christmas and her babies from the wolf. She proved herself unselfish. She definitely earned the right to be a Guardian Angel Dog."

Aurora said to Sandy, "Seems Rivers is barkless with the news that you are a Guardian Angel Dog, Sandy."

"Yes, you sure are on a roll here, Aurora, with surprises for Rivers. You may as well tell him the rest of the news," Sandy replied, chuckling.

"Well Sandy, if you insist. Rivers, Sandy has been assigned as your Guardian Angel Dog." Before I could utter a sound, Aurora said, "She is also the Guardian Angel Dog for Christmas and her pups, plus all of your teammates."

I am not used to being barkless, but that sure was the case tonight. Wow, Sandy is our Guardian Angel Dog. The team and especially Christmas would be very surprised when I told them about that.

"Sorry Rivers, you cannot tell them." It was Sandy. I forgot, Guardian Angel Dogs could read our thoughts. "All of your buddies, including Christmas and her babies, will be visited by us tonight. Our visit with them will be real, but they may think it is a dream. They will need to decide if they want to believe in their Guardian Angel Dog. Just like you did, when you called upon Aurora for help."

Aurora added. "It is called faith, believing in something you cannot see and your senses tell you does not exists. Your teammates need to make their own decisions, if they want to believe or not."

Barkless and confused. Yes, I believe in my Guardian Angel Dog and I want my teammates to believe also. It is so comforting to know that when you have that uphill climb and the trail gets tough, you have some extra dog power to help you crest the hill.

"Rivers." It was Sandy. "You cannot do this for your teammates, they must do this on their own. Understand?"

"Yes," I said weakly. "But I really want my teammates to believe."

Aurora said. "That is up to them. We will do our part, but they have to decide. Some already do believe, others do not, and some never will. You are a dog of your bark. Will you give us your bark that you will not tell them?" I nodded yes and then Aurora added, "Good. Come Sandy, we have to get to work."

"Wait!" I said. "What about Sunny, is Sandy her Guardian Angel Dog?" I asked.

Sandy answered. "Any dog that joins Mike's team, or lives in Mike's home, or stays in your yard is included. That means Sunny, the puppies, and the new dog, who will come to live with you shortly. However, they must decide to believe in their Guardian Angel Dog. Otherwise, we can do nothing special to help them, except to watch over them."

When Sandy finished, I knew they left to visit my teammates. As I wandered back to my doghouse, I had many mixed feelings, and had no one I could bark to about them. I was very happy that Sandy was our Guardian Angel Dog. However, I was sad because some of my teammates might decide not to believe. I could not help them. I gave my bark and if I went back on my bark, I would have no honor and would disgrace my Husky heritage. I guess this is like choosing between right and wrong. I stopped walking and howled a prayer into the night that all of them would make the right decision.

After morning chow, Christmas and her three puppies, Tundra, Stormy, and Sky, visited with me. Christmas told the pups that since my teammates and I were Christmas' uncles, we were also the pups' uncles as well. We would help teach the pups, just as we taught and looked after Christmas.

Uncle Nitro teaches them to be brave and to protect each other. Uncle Brownie teaches them to be honest and to better themselves. Uncle Ugly teaches them to laugh at themselves and not take themselves too seriously. Uncle Doc teaches them to be great lead dogs, and the academic things dogs needs to know. Uncle Lakota teaches them to be respectful towards others, as well as to themselves, and to think before they act. And me? Well, I guess I teach them about life.

"Hi," I said, as I heard them come near me.

"Uncle Rivers." It was Christmas and I knew she had something on her mind. "I had this dream that Aunt Sandy and another dog named Aurora were talking to me about Guardian Angel Dogs. They told me that Aunt Sandy was my Guardian Angel Dog. Then

this morning, my babies told me they had the same dream. Isn't that strange?" Christmas asked.

I heard them sit down around me, waiting for my answer. "I don't know. Do you think it is strange?" I asked.

Before Christmas could answer, Tundra said. "Mama, it was no dream. I saw tears in Aunt Sandy eyes, as she nuzzled me just like she did before she…"

Tundra's voice trembled, filled with emotions. Sandy played with them as if they were her own babies. I heard that the pups saw the wolf and …

Sky's words interrupted my thoughts. "Tundra is right, Mama. It was no dream. I felt Aunt Sandy also, and Aurora touched me with her paw as she talked to me. They were real. I believe that Aunt Sandy is right here watching over me."

"Me too," said Stormy. "I know that Aunt Sandy will be there protecting me just like she did with the wolf. I believe that Aunt Sandy will always look after us."

I knew I had not answered Christmas' questions but her babies were doing a good job telling her about their beliefs. "Christmas," I said. "I cannot answer your question. However, I do know that things happen in our lives that we can never explain. Who knows, maybe you were being watched over and guided the night we found you."

"Sometimes, Christmas, it is better to think with your heart and not with your head." I said. "Sometimes our heads do not let us see the purity of the issue that our hearts know is there."

In a very soft and gentle voice, Christmas asked me, "Do you believe that you have a Guardian Angel Dog?"

I answered, "What I believe should not matter to you. What I believe should not affect whether you believe the dream was a dream or real, as your babies say it is. However, I will tell you that I believe Sandy is in a place where if I am in trouble she will help me."

When I stopped talking, Christmas started to speak. Her voice was relaxed and she sounded relieved. I bet she had made her decision. "Uncle Rivers, you make a lot of sense. Thank you." Then I heard her turn to her pups and say, "Time to go and clean up the doghouses."

As I heard them scamper off, I smiled to myself as I remembered that Sandy used to say the same words to Christmas when she was a puppy!

The Sourdough 120

Mike is not a racer. He mushes us for fun. Nevertheless, he knows that since we are all retired racers, and experienced the thrill of racing, we never lost the desire to race. So, we hoped that when racing season came around, Mike would consider racing us. Nitro reminded us that Mike had said he was getting another dog or two to fill out the team for the racing season. Yes, the summer was a long season of anticipation for snow and the race season.

I bet you can imagine how excited we were when Mike told us he was going to race us in the Sourdough 120. Well, I was excited. Nitro was ecstatic! While this race is not as long as we were used to, it is a race and that was all that counted.

The Sourdough 120 was a race done in two segments: 60 miles one way, an overnight stop at the checkpoint and then the 60 miles back to the start. It was a novice or beginners' race since there was a lot of supervision on the trail. It was an open class race, which meant that there was no age limit. You only needed at least ten dogs, a sled, some gear, and the desire to have some fun.

Some experienced racers used the Sourdough as a tune-up for bigger races. Others used it to check out their dogs. Some mushers used the race to decide if they really wanted to be racers. And then there were mushers like Mike, who would do this race for their dogs. Yep, Mike was giving us what might be our final chance to compete, and the only time he might race with us. Wow, this was going to be special.

Wait a minute. We only had seven dogs: my five teammates, Christmas, and me. So you can bet that I was relieved when Mike told us that he planned to run Sky, Tundra and Storm.

Sure, the pups were young, but they had six very experienced uncles who would not only train them but also take care of them on the trail. While Christmas had never raced, she had proved herself on the trails. Yes, this was going to be a fun run, a family fun run. While only the pups and Christmas were related, we considered ourselves a family. Besides, you know what they say, "The family that runs the trails together has fun together!"

So now we had our team, the ten dogs we needed to enter the Sourdough. We had our sled, the new one that Mark at the Grateful Sled had hand made for us. In addition, Mike owned all of the equipment we needed to run this race.

I must admit that I was surprised to see how determined Mike was to get us ready for this race. Each day we ran farther and farther on the trail until we were doing very long runs. Then Mike took us to train on the actual race trail. We all took our turn running lead and became familiar with the race trail. Sometimes we did overnight trips to get used to being out and getting our break-camp routine down pat.

The pups, Tundra, Storm and Sky were doing very well. Lakota told me that you could see the pride in Christmas' face. She knew her babies were growing up to be fine sled dogs.

Doc told me that the pups looked exceptionally strong and ran very well. Yes, they made us proud. Too bad they were a bit too young to realize that they were a true credit to their Husky heritage.

And my buddies, Nitro, Doc, Lakota, Brownie and Ugly, were running like young dogs, excited to race and compete, listening for and obeying Mike's commands, perfectly. Yes, I was proud of my buddies. We were a team! A good team. A team that would not let Mike down.

Many times Randy came with us. Mike would run the team out and Randy would run us back home. Mike did this so that we would not become solely dependent on him, but rather on each other, thus functioning better as a team.

Randy was young and becoming a very good musher. He loved to mush and took very good care of us on the trail. Randy gained more and more confidence with each run. Moreover, that confidence was not just limited to his mushing, but also affected his schoolwork and writing. His stories improved with each one he wrote. Many times when we camped out, he would read his stories to us. Randy was becoming very much like Mike when it came to us. He talked to us and gave us great ear rubs. He cared for us and he was our buddy. We all liked him. We hoped that someday Mike would let Randy race us. As it turned out, that day came sooner than we would ever have imagined.

The day was perfect for training. We were in our team positions with Doc and Christmas in lead. Sky and Stormy were in the swing position. Lakota and I were in the wheel position. Nitro, Brownie, Ugly, and Tundra were team dogs. Mike loaded the sled with all of the equipment and food needed for an overnight trip. He told us we were going far up the trail, past the planned race checkpoint. We would camp overnight, and then head on back. This would be a good tune-up for the race, which was only a few weeks away.

Mike was on the runners and Randy was in the basket. We were comfortable in our stride. We were working together as one, an extension of Mike running the team. Lakota was telling me all about the trail. He said that the trail was becoming narrower.

I smelled it just as Mike yelled, "Team Stop!" We stopped as Mike said, "Randy, get out of the basket and stand behind the sled." Then I heard Mike unzip the sled bag.

Bear is what I smelled. Lakota told me that a huge bear was blocking the trail. It was eating and we had disturbed it. Nitro added that the bear was very upset that we were in its territory, especially when it was eating. Nitro also mentioned that there was no way to get around the bear, and he was approaching us.

Lakota told me that Mike had his gun and was in front of the lead dogs. I heard him fire one shot. Lakota told that the shot hit the ground between the bear's legs. A warning shot. It did not work. Doc said that it only served to aggravate the bear. It kept on coming towards us.

"Randy," Mike said. "Cut the dogs loose and head them back down the trail."

"But Mister Mike."

"No buts, Randy. Just do it."

I heard Randy cut the main gang line and call Doc, Christmas and the pups to him, I felt the gang line pull taut as the dogs made a U turn and headed back down the trail.

"I'm not going. It was Nitro. "Me too." That was Brownie. Doc and Ugly joined in and so did Lakota. I would stand with Mike also.

"Team. Go." Mike said. No, we stayed. Lakota told me that

Randy was confused but cut the gang line again by Doc and moved Christmas with her pups behind the sled.

The bear kept coming down the trail toward us. We started to bark, but it kept on coming. Then I heard Mike's gun. Bam, Bam. But the bear kept coming. Bam. Bam. Lakota told me that Mike shot the bear four times but the bear kept coming and was almost on top of Mike. Bam, another shot. I heard the bear fall down.

Ugly said that the bear clobbered Mike and knocked him down before Mike got off the last shot.

"Mister Mike?" It was Randy. "Are you okay?"

"Randy, where are my glasses? I cannot see without them."

"I found them Mister Mike, but they are shattered."

Lakota told me that Mike tried to get up, but we heard him groan and clutch his right arm. "Randy, I think the bear broke my arm when he hit me. You are going to have to splint it and get us home."

"Mister Mike, what do I need to do? I was surprised at the calmness in Randy's voice.

"I would suggest that we get the dogs secured first. After that get the first aid kit out of the sled and I will try to help you splint my arm. Then we have to unload the sled and move it back down the trail, then reload it. It is starting to get dark, so I hope you feel comfortable mushing at night. It will be a first for you. Nothing like learning under fire," Mike said.

After Randy got Mike's arm splinted, he started to retie the gang line and hook us up.

"Where is Doc?" Randy asked. I heard the dogs look around but they told me they could not see him. Wait, I heard a groan coming from the bear. It cannot still be alive. Oh no, that is not the bear. Is it Doc?

"Doc, where are you?" I asked.

"I am under the bear, it fell on me. I am hurt. I need help," Doc said.

I started to bark and pull towards the bear.

"Randy, check by the bear and see if it fell on Doc. Rivers is barking. Maybe he hears something," Mike said.

Lakota told me that Randy ran to the side of the bear that fell towards the team.

"Yes, Mister Mike. Doc is under the bear. I cannot get him out, the bear too heavy," Randy said.

"Okay Randy. Brownie told me that Mike got up and rushed over to where Randy was. From what Mike said, Doc was just under the bear's chest. Mike told Randy that they would use the dogs to pull the bear off Doc. He told Randy to tie a rope to the bear's forepaw and then move us down the trail in the direction the bear came from. We then would pull the bear back down the trail, and away from our sled and off of Doc.

After Randy repositioned the team and hitched us to the bear, he gave us the "Hike, Hike" command and we pulled. Brownie told me this was a big bear, but it seemed very light to pull… or was it that we were very anxious to get it off our teammate Doc?

Once Randy saw that we had the bear off Doc, he told us to stop. Then I heard him race back to where Mike was, to help with Doc.

Lakota told me that they were both on the ground near Doc.

"Is he going to be okay, Mister Mike?" Randy asked. You could tell he was very concerned.

"I don't know," Mike said. "Doc is breathing okay, but he is very tender around his hips. I think the snow acted as a pillow so that the bear did not squash Doc. However, he is hurt. I am not sure if he has any internal damage. We need to get him back home very quickly."

After Randy repositioned the sled and hooked the team to it, Mike got into the basket and cradled Doc in his lap. They wrapped Doc in a sleeping bag. I tried to talk to him. He was in pain. I told him we would get him home and he would be okay.

Randy got on the runners. Lakota told me that both Mike and Randy wore their headlamps. We headed back down the trail towards home.

Christmas was still in lead. Ugly was her co-leader. Nitro ran as a solo swing dog. Sky, Storm, Brownie and Tundra were in the team dog positions. Lakota and I ran the wheel.

We raced home. We were worried that Mike and Doc would be jostled in the sled basket. The mood of the team was some-what somber. We needed Doc for the race since he was our leader, our friend, and our teammate. If Mike had a broken arm, he could not race and then we could not either. Bummer, as Christmas would say.

Mike helped Randy navigate the trails home. Randy was do-ing a great job running the team. We were racing very fast, faster than Randy had ever run with us. He was mushing well

under pressure. I am sure he was as concerned about Mike and Doc as we were.

"Uncle Rivers." It was Christmas. "Is Mike okay?" Christmas had become very devoted and very close to Mike, especially since the puppies were born. I know she was very concerned. While Christmas and the rest of the team were concerned about Doc, they were not saying much. Before I answered her, I got off a fast howl to Sandy, asking that both Doc and Mike would be okay.

"Mike is comfortable and talking to Randy, Christmas." I said. "I think he will be okay. Doc is resting comfortably and his breathing sounds okay."

"Thanks, Uncle Rivers." Christmas sounded relieved.

When we got closer to home, Mike called Doctor Jim on the cell phone. I heard Mike tell Doctor Jim what had happened. Mike asked Doctor Jim to meet us at our home with his mobile vet office.

Randy asked Mike why he did not use the cell phone and call sooner. Mike replied that we were out of range. He had to wait until we were closer to our home for the cell phone to work.

Doctor Jim was at our home when we got there. Lakota told me Doctor Jim took Doc from Mike. "Are you okay, Uncle Doc?" It was Tundra.

"I will be okay Tunny, don't worry." Doc had given Tundra the nickname Tunny and every time Doc called her that, you knew she felt special.

"Mike, you need to get your arm checked by a doctor. I will take care of Doc," Doctor Jim said. I could tell Mike did not want to go, but Mary insisted and took Mike to the hospital to check out his arm. Randy took care of our equipment and us. As he fed and watered us, Randy talked to us, letting us know he was worried about Mike and Doc. We all nuzzled him to let him know that we were proud of him and the great job he did getting us home. Nitro mentioned to me that he was very impressed and proud of Randy, since he did not cave under the pressure. For a young boy, Randy handled this accident with a lot of maturity.

Ugly told me he found a tennis ball in the yard and dropped it by Randy. "You want to play Catch and Fetch, Ugly?" Randy asked. With that, Randy picked up the ball and threw it in the yard for Ugly to fetch. But instead of just Ugly chasing after the

ball, all the dogs, except Lakota and I went after it. I guess it must have looked very funny since Randy started to laugh. Lakota told me that all the dogs were chasing after the ball. They would tackle the dog who had it, making the dog drop the ball. Then the dogs would chase the dog who picked it up. Lakota told me that Nitro had the ball and both Sky and Stormy were chasing him to get it. Lakota told me that both pups ran right into Nitro and bounced off him because he is so big. However, before the pups realized it, Nitro dropped the ball and pretended that they knocked him down. I heard Stormy and Sky laugh as they wrestled for the ball.

I heard a truck drive up into the driveway and Lakota told me that it was our truck with Mike and Mary. Lakota said that Doc was with them. He was walking but Lakota said you could tell he was not well.

We all gathered around the gate as Mike and Doc came by. Brownie told me that Mike had a white thing on his arm just like what Sunny had on her leg. That is not a good sign.

"Mister Mike, are you and Doc okay?" Randy asked.

"Well, Doc is a bit shaken up and needs to rest for a few weeks. Fortunately, there is no internal damage from the bear falling on him. He has no broken bones, but he is sore and tender in the hips. Me, I have a broken arm, which means I cannot race the team in the Sourdough 120," Mike said.

Oh no, I thought, we are not going to race. It was starting to set in that all of the training and preparation for the race was over, when Mike interrupted my thoughts with, "Randy, I cannot race, but you can."

Before Randy could answer Mike added, "We will need another dog since Doc may not be able to race. I talked to my good friend GB Jones and he told me I could borrow Fin. Rivers and Fin have run together so that should help out some."

"Mister Mike," Randy said, "Do you really think I can do the race?"

"Randy, it is not what I think, it is what you believe," Mike said.

Silence. Lakota told me that all eyes were on Randy. I know what we wanted the answer to be. Even the pups were sitting watching Randy. Brownie and Ugly went over to Randy and nuzzled his hand, telling him what his answer needed to be,

"Well Randy, will you race my team in the race?"

"Yes, Mister Mike, I really want to do this," was Randy's answer.

Racing for Randy

The time from the bear strike to the start of the race flew by. Fin joined us and meshed right in as a member of our team. Randy took us out for short runs with Mike in the basket. Randy spent a lot of time with us, practicing our setup and break-camp routines. Randy could stop the team, check our paws, then feed and water us very quickly. This is very important when racing. The more time it takes you to get back on the trail, the longer it will take you to get to the finish line.

In addition, the faster Randy could get us fed, watered, and checked would give him more time to rest. You only have so much time available in the checkpoints. A good routine does wonders to make checkpoint time go smoothly.

When we were in the kennel practicing, Doc would be on the sidelines barking encouragement to us and passing on tips to the pups. We all knew that he wanted to go, but he never showed his disappointment that he could not race with us. That is Doc, the leader, always thinking of his teammates.

Christmas told me that Tundra was sad that Doc would not be racing with us. From what Christmas told me, Doc was a major influence in Tundra's life. Doc was her hero. I told Christmas that it was great that Tundra had a hero and she could not have picked a better one.

What is that expression? Time flies when you are having fun. Yes, it sure does. While Mike did have a broken arm, he managed to do many things around the yard. One thing was to drive us to the race starting point.

Mike made a checklist of what to pack in the truck, and Randy got it all loaded, except for us.

"Okay Mister Mike, the truck is loaded," Randy said. "I am going to start putting the dogs into their dog boxes."

Mike answered, "Let me help you." Mike called us and we all walked to the truck. I walked with Lakota, who guided me. As we walked, I heard footsteps lagging behind us and Lakota told me that Doc was following us and he had his harness in his mouth.

"Mister Mike, look, it is Doc walking with the team to the truck. He has his harness with him," Randy said.

I heard Mike laugh as he walked over to where I knew Doc was. The team stopped. Lakota told me that Mike knelt next to Doc and rubbed his ears as Doc dropped his harness by Mike's feet. Doc sat as Mike talked to him.

"Doc," Mike said, "Doctor Jim said he did not want you to run for a while. You know, to make sure you are okay, after the bear fell on you."

Lakota told me that Doc looked at Mike. Doc licked Mike's hand that belonged to the arm in the white thing. Doc then got up, picked up his harness, walked around Mike, and got in front of the team. Lakota told me that Doc was now the lead dog in our march to the truck. He looked back at the team and barked, "Lets go team, and look sharp. We are racing for Randy and we are committed to giving him our best in this race. Let's go to the truck."

After Doc finished talking to us, he turned and walked to the truck, right to the dog box that had his name on it. We all fell in step and followed.

"Yippee!" It was Tundra. "Uncle Doc is racing with us."

"Maybe not," Sky said. "Mike has not agreed to that yet."

Tundra said, "Well not yet but he will." Lakota told me that Tundra walked back to where Mike was kneeling and started to bark at him.

As Tundra barked, Mike laughed. Randy started to laugh also. Lakota told me that it was very funny watching Tundra dance around Mike barking at him. She used different tones in her barking. One tone was pleading, and another tone was debating. She was very good at this.

Soon, Lakota told me that Mike got up, gave Tundra an ear rub, and told her to get back in the line. I heard Mike walk past me to where I knew Doc was. Lakota told me that Doc was sitting very patiently by the truck.

Lakota told me that Mike opened the door and Doc jumped up. Mike helped him into the box. Randy was there also.

"Okay Doc, you can race with the team. However, I am telling you in front of Randy and the team that if you show any signs of soreness or favoring those hips, Randy will yank you out of the line and you will ride in the basket. You understand, Doc? We do not want you to be crippled. You have nothing to prove here. You are a true champion, so do not take chances that will endanger your running with your teammates again. That, my friend, would not be fair to your buddies."

Doc barked once, agreeing to what Mike said.

"Randy, it looks like you have an 11 dog team for this race. Doc will run solo lead with Christmas and Brownie in the swing position. That will give you three lead dogs up front. Next, run Stormy and Sky then Tundra with Ugly. Nitro and Fin will run together, so that leaves Rivers and Lakota in the wheel."

Mike kept talking as Randy worked to put us in our dog boxes. "That setup will make sure that there is very little pressure on Doc to pull. Keep in mind that he is stubborn and proud. He probably will not give you any clear sign that he hurts. Use your instincts and watch the other dogs. Both will give you a good indication if you need to pull Doc. If you do, bring him home in the basket. Do not drop him at the checkpoint. You have plenty of power to give him a free ride for the entire race. If he wants to run this one so much, then he deserves to finish it."

"Speaking of power," Mike said, I have never told you my magic word. If you yell the magic word at this team, they will give you a blinding burst of speed and power that you might need to get out of a jam. Use it only in an emergency. The magic word is 'Banshee.' For some unknown reason that word that just cranks them up. However, it does drain them so use it only in an emergency. Understand, Randy?"

"Yes Mister Mike, and thanks for letting Doc run the race with us. I was hoping he would be able to."

"Well, Randy, you need to thank Tundra. She convinced me, when she started to bark on Doc's behalf. That surprised me."

"Momma, did I do something wrong when I barked at Mike to let Doc race with us?" Tundra asked her mother, Christmas.

"No honey, you did a very good thing. I am proud of you," Christmas said.

"And so am I, Tunny. Thank you," Doc said.

"By the way, Mister Mike, what is a Banshee?" Randy asked.

"I think it is an Irish witch," Mike replied.

"Hmmm, maybe your dogs are Irish Alaskan Huskies." Randy said as he started to laugh.

"Now you are a comic, Randy?" Mike said as he laughed.

The talk stopped. The truck started. We were on our way.

We'll Be Home Tomorrow

It was a beautiful day for racing: great temperatures and fresh snow, which just made race day even more exciting. While my buddies and I had been through the excitement of starting before, Christmas and her pups had not. We let them jump and bark, but we did rein them in a bit, but still allowed them to enjoy these exciting moments of their first race. Running 60 miles on a trail is one thing. Racing 60 miles is another, and you need every bit of your resources to get the job done. Yes, it is a job, but one that we all love.

Randy put our harnesses on us. Lakota told me that we had changed team colors from Mike's green and gold to Randy's red and blue. Mike had also given Randy a new, smaller sled made by Mark at the Grateful Sled. While the new sled was as long as Mike's, the driving bow was shorter to accommodate Randy, who is a lot shorter than Mike. We had practiced with this sled and I can tell you it was fast and light. The shorter driving bow fit Randy perfectly and he could drive this sled very easily. Lakota told me that there was a new red and blue sled bag with Randy's name stitched in it.

After Randy put us in harness and in our team positions, Mike came to us and talked to us while Randy slipped into the truck for a few minutes.

"Team," Mike said very softly so that only we could hear him. "I am very proud of you and the way you committed to Randy for his first race. I wish I could be driving you in this one, but it looks like our day for racing together will have to wait. Nevertheless, it will come and I promise you that we will all race together someday." I noticed a bit of sadness in Mike's voice.

"Nitro," Mike called out, "while you may not be the lead dog today or tomorrow, you are the one in charge of making sure

111

that Randy is safe. I am sure some of the teams out there might not play by the rules. Your job, Nitro, is to make sure that Randy does not get hurt, and lead him out of trouble if there is any."

Nitro barked that he understood.

"Brownie," Mike said, "I want you to keep an eye on Doc. You and Christmas need to keep the pulling weight off him. Moreover, if you think he is hurting, let Randy know. Christmas will help you do that, but she also needs to keep watch over her pups since this is their first race."

Brownie barked that he knew what Mike expected of him.

"Christmas, "Mike said. "I am asking a lot of you in your first race. Pull some of Doc's load, watch over your babies and help lead. I know you can do it. You, like the rest of the team, have shown me you are a true champion and a credit to your Husky heritage."

Lakota told me that Christmas licked Mike's check. Yes, there was a special bond developing between Mike and Christmas, just as Sandy had said there would be.

"Ugly," Mike called out. "I want you to help Christmas with the pups. Make sure that they do not get into trouble or mischief. They are good dogs, but they are young and may want to play. Help Christmas to keep them focused. Okay?"

Ugly barked. While Ugly might be the joke master among us, the pups knew that when Ugly was serious, play time was over.

I heard Mike give Fin some special encouragement also. Fin deserved it. He had worked very hard with us for this race. I hoped he would race with us again.

"Lakota," Mike said, "I need you to help Nitro to protect Randy on the trail. I know you are shy, but I also know you are very protective of your teammates, the pups and me. I am asking you to do the same for Randy. Okay?"

Lakota barked and told me he was surprised to hear what Mike asked him to do, but he, like the rest of us, was devoted to Mike and would do whatever Mike asked. I knew that between Nitro and Lakota, no harm would come to Randy.

I heard Mike come over to me. He put his hands on each side of my face and whispered very softly that he was proud of me and to have a great time with this race. He promised me our racing day would come. Yes Mike, I know it will and I will be there for you as you have been there for me since we met.

I heard Randy come out of the truck and Lakota told me he

had on a new blue and red storm suit. They were the same colors as his sled bag.

"Mister Mike," Randy said. "Thank you for the new storm suit, but my old suit was still good. I did not need a new one."

"Yes Randy, I know, but I wanted your first race to be special so I got you one that matches your team colors."

Mike said, "Randy, I want to talk to you about this race before you get started. I found out that Dylan Crawford is running in this race. He is a bully and picks on the smaller racers. He likes to steal stuff while mushers are sleeping." He has been caught several times, but no one pressed the issue because Dylan's dad, Mister Crawford, is a real bad character."

"I will be okay Mister Mike, you have no need to worry," Randy said, but I noticed the concern in Randy's voice.

"I am sure you can take care of yourself, Randy, but I want to give you some ideas that will make taking care of yourself a bit easier. Okay?"

Mike continued, "First, try to break or rest in places where other mushers are present. I doubt if Dylan will try anything if there are a lot of others present. When you camp for the night at the checkpoint, try to bed down near GB Jones or Stan Smith. GB is the race marshal and Stan is helping with monitoring the racers. Both are friends of mine and know you are racing our team."

"When you bed down for the night, move Nitro and Lakota together, and bed down by them. Also, move all of the equipment to one side of the sled. Let Doc sleep in the sled basket on the extra blanket. Besides helping Doc rest after the run, he will start barking if anyone comes near the basket, that is if Rivers does not hear him first and warn you and the other dogs."

Mike told Randy, "I understand that Dylan is not too, uh, bright. So just use your wits and avoid trouble. It might be smart to let him stay ahead of you. That way you can keep an eye on him. Let him beat you to the finish line. Winning is not the most important thing here. The important thing is to run a good race by the rules, display sportsmanship and take care of your dogs and yourself."

"Okay Mister Mike, I understand and will do as you ask," Randy replied. His voice sounded more confident, now that he had an idea of what to do to avoid a problem with Dylan.

"Team 7, you have two minutes." Lakota told me that seven was our number. Wow, this was going to be an interesting race after

all. Bad guys on the trail, Christmas' and the pups' first race, Doc not up to 100 percent and Randy racing for the first time. Who knew what else we would run into.

We moved into the starting chute. Randy came by each one of us and gave us a big hug. We were ready. I heard the time-keeper say "30 seconds." Lakota told me that Randy made a last minute check of our lines and harnesses.

"Fifteen seconds" and I heard Randy get on the runners.

"Five" and I heard the pups bark with excitement. They were ready to go.

"Four" and Doc yelled that this was just like old times. He was one happy dog!

"Three" and Lakota asked me if I was ready. "Yes," I replied. "Let's rock!"

"Two" and Randy yells," Team ready!"

"One" and then Randy's "Hike. Hike." We all leaned into our harnesses and took off down the trail. The race was on, and so was this adventure. And the last voice I heard from the cheering crowd was Mike's: "Be safe and have fun."

His Time Has Come Today!

The trail was very fast and we were making good time. Doc's strategy was to use the first few miles to get our stride and pace ourselves. He wanted to see what the other teams had. Our plan was to finish in good standing, get the pups, Christmas and Randy some race experience, and have a good time.

After a mile or so, the pups settled down and started to work with us in the team. We talked to them and they told us they were really enjoying this. I know that Tundra was watching every move Doc made and listening to every word Doc barked. She was very intent on learning from her hero.

The sled was a breeze to pull. It was very nimble and Randy was doing a great job of driving it. While we carried a lot more gear than was required, we had no trouble moving the sled at a very fast pace.

The pups surprised us by how powerful they were. Lakota told me that Doc's tug lines were barely taut, meaning that he was not pulling much weight. That is what Mike wanted, but I did not think Mike expected the pups to want to pull more than their share.

No teams passed us on the trail, which might have meant that all the other teams were holding back and would make their move tomorrow, after we had left the checkpoint. This is an experienced musher's strategy. I guessed the rookies were learning from the experienced mushers. Nitro wished he knew what position this Dylan character had started in. Was he in front of us or behind us?

The miles glided by and before we knew it, we were at the checkpoint for the overnight stay. After we pulled off the trail,

the race officials checked our gear, to make sure we had all of the required stuff, and the trail vets gave us the once-over. They told Randy we all were okay, and told him where to set up camp for the night. Randy asked them if Dylan had come into the checkpoint. No, they told Randy, Dylan had not checked in yet. That meant he was behind us. Nitro was not happy with that.

Randy set up camp. He made a fire in the camp stove and cooked us a hot meal. Sure tasted like Mary's cooking...

Randy said, "Ms. Mary made us some special chow for the trail. Told me to make sure you all cleaned your bowls. So, please do that so I can tell her, and make her happy. You know she loves to cook for all of us. And she made me something special also."

Lakota took his head out of his bowl long enough to tell me that Randy sat down near us and was really enjoying his chow. Ugly made a comment that Randy was sure enjoying his food. "You would think the kid never ate, by the way he is devouring his meal."

We all figured that Randy did not eat well at the foster home. We guessed that was why Mike and Mary always scheduled chow time for when Randy was with us. Christmas told me that Mary always gave Randy a basket of food before he returned to the foster home.

After we ate, Randy gave us all a lot of individual attention and TLC. You could bet your last dog biscuit that we heaped a bunch of TLC on him also. After that, we just loafed. Ugly was telling some joke, while Nitro was telling bedtime stories to the pups, just like he used to do for Christmas.

I heard the sled pull into the checkpoint. Then I head several voices that were arguing. I could not make out what the voices were saying at first, but it sounded like a very intense argument. It became louder and I heard Musher GB and Musher Stan. Apparently, the musher who came into the checkpoint refused to let the vets check his dogs. I heard Musher GB tell the musher that if the vets did not check his dogs, the musher would be disqualified.

"Dylan, I am warning you for the last time. Let the vets check your dogs or else I will disqualify you from the race." That was Musher GB.

So, Dylan was behind us. I told Nitro and all of the dogs to keep quiet so I could hear what was going on.

"GB." It was Musher Stan. "These dogs have fresh welts on their rumps, and there is a jiggle stick with a strap attached to it on the top of the sled bag. These dogs have been whipped!" I could hear the anger in Musher Stan's voice.

"Did you beat these dogs, Dylan?" Musher GB asked.

"None of your business, they are my dogs," Dylan replied.

"True, but dog beating is illegal and I will report you to the State Troopers," Musher GB added. "Consider yourself disqualified from this race. Park your sled and I will have the vets tend to your dogs.

"No way, old man," Dylan yelled. "Hike, Hike." Then I heard the sled take off down the trail.

"You want me to go after him, GB?" Musher Stan asked.

"No, he has to show up back at the starting point in order to get home. I will call the troopers and ask them to be there in case he shows up before we do. He will have to stop to rest. By the looks of it, his team is in very bad shape and will lie down on him before long." Musher GB continued, "Let's tell the other mushers to keep an eye out for Dylan on the trail, but also warn them that he may cause them trouble."

In a short while, Musher Stan and Musher GB came by our camp to tell us about Dylan. Randy thanked them and told them that he had known Dylan was on the trail. Randy told Musher GB and Musher Stan that Mike had told him what precautions to take.

"You do what Mike told you to do, Randy," Musher Stan said. "But if you need any help or have any trouble, just call out. I am camped a little ways down the trail from you."

"Thank you Mister Stan, I will do that. Think I want to turn in now. I am kind of tired," Randy said.

Good night Randy," Musher GB said. "Have a good race." I heard their footsteps fade in the night as they walked the trail to another team.

Bark about an interesting night. Lakota told me that Randy moved Doc into the sled basket as Mike had suggested, and then put Tundra in there also.

"Doc," Randy said, "you did very well today, but I know you pushed yourself the last few miles. I know you are very tired so I am putting Tundra in the basket also. You rest while she guards the gear. Besides being a great watchdog, I know Tundra will like being near you tonight. Just do not tell her too many trail stories. You need your rest."

Nitro told us that Randy moved the team into a circle instead of a straight line. Nitro said that Randy moved all of our gear to

the center of the circle and laid out his sleeping bag by the gear. From the way Nitro described it, anyone or anything that wanted to steal our gear or bother Randy had to get through the ring of dogs. Nitro then told me that Randy took Lakota and Nitro out of the team and told them to stay by the gear and sleeping bag. That way, even if someone or something did get past the ring of dogs, they would have to deal with Nitro and Lakota, the team's biggest dogs, while still having the ring of dogs around them.

This was very smart. I started to wonder how Randy came up with this idea. I heard Sky and Stormy talking and they said "musk ox."

"Musk ox?" I asked.

"Yes, Uncle Rivers," Sky said. "When musk ox fear they will be attacked, they stand shoulder to shoulder and form a tight circle around their young. They face out toward the attacker. Musk ox are very big, so the attacker can not get into the circle, because they can not get past the musk ox."

"Oh," I said. "How did you know that?" I asked.

Stormy replied, "Randy told us. Actually, when we were smaller and could not run with you, Randy would read to us. He told us that he was practicing his reading so that he could speak and read better. Randy said it was fun to read to us because if he made a mistake, we would not make fun of him. He wanted Mike to be proud of him, since Mike had encouraged him to read and write stories."

"So," Sky added, "he read to us about the musk ox and how they live in herds."

Then Stormy added, "It looks like he remembered them, and decided that the circle would be a great way to protect us tonight, especially with that Dylan boy out there."

Son of a dog! Randy read to the pups. No wonder they had learned so fast. Mike told Randy to use his wits and I bet Mike would be very proud of how Randy was doing just that.

Before Randy crawled into his sleeping bag, Brownie told me that Randy repositioned the dogs. Fin and Christmas were the lead dogs. Brownie and Sky were in the swing dog positions. Ugly and Stormy came next. The next position was empty since Nitro was inside the circle and Tundra was in the basket. I figured Randy would team them together. Lakota, who was also in the circle, would run with me. I had a hunch that Doc would get to ride the basket home.

"Doc," Randy said. "You are riding home in the basket tomorrow. I do not want to take a chance on hurting you if I have to run the team very fast because of problems. I know Mike is proud of you for racing this far with us. Thank you."

Ugly told me that Doc just nuzzled Randy. "It is okay, team," Doc said. "Randy is right. This was a very smart decision he made. I want to lead you across the finish line, but my musher and my team must come before what I want to do. Christmas and Fin will do a great job of getting you home and keeping you out of trouble if necessary."

Doc continues to amaze me. He is a true leader, in additional to being great friend.

I heard Randy crawl into his sleeping bag, and then both Nitro and Lakota lay down near Randy, probably curled up to him.

It was a peaceful dream. I was lying on fresh straw with a gentle breeze keeping the mosquitoes from bothering me. That is, it was peaceful until Tundra's barking woke me. I stood up, as did every other dog in the team. I heard footsteps. They stopped. Ugly told me that first Tundra and then Doc were barking in the direction of the woods across the trail from us. There was someone or something out there. Let me rephrase that... someone.

"Who is out there?" a voice yelled. No, it was not Randy's voice; he was being very quiet. There was no answer. I heard the footsteps get softer as they faded away into the night. I told the team that whoever it was had left our area.

"Tunny." It was Doc. "You did very good job young lady, warning us about the stranger in the woods. I bet you saved us."

"You okay Tundra?" It was her mother, Christmas. "Oh yes, Momma, I heard someone or something walking towards us. I did not recognize the scent, so I knew it was not Musher Stan or Musher GB. So I started to bark."

"As Uncle Doc said, you did a very good job. Now settle down Tundra, and get some rest. Tomorrow will be a big day."

"Yes Momma, good night," Tundra said. You knew she was just beaming with pride that her Uncle Doc and her mother told her she did a good thing.

The rest of the night was uneventful and I figured it was first light when Randy got up, fixed us some hot chow, and got the team and gear ready for the run home. We heard other teams talk about a dog and some equipment that were missing. I wondered if Tundra's barking saved us from an unexpected and

unwanted visitor. I bet Randy's circle not only protected him and us, but also confused the visitor. The intruder would expect a stung-out dog team, not a circle of dogs.

We broke camp and started back down the trail. We now entered our racing mode. The trail was fast and we raced along at a good pace. The hours and miles melted away. None of us was tiring. We actually were getting stronger, anticipating the finish of this race.

Lakota told me that the trail was wide enough for two dog teams to pass each other. So when another team came up behind us, I was not surprised that Randy did not move over to let them pass. What did surprise me was that the musher stayed behind us and yelling insults at Randy.

Why would a musher not want to pass us, and continue to insult Randy? Dylan!! It had to be him. Wanting to cause trouble, and try to steal our equipment. Maybe even steal one of us.

This was becoming scary.

Randy slowed us down a bit to let the other team pass. Randy probably thought the other musher just wanted to pass. Randy did not know what Dylan looked like.

Doc told us that the trail narrowed about a quarter mile up the trail, and we had about 2 miles to the finish line. Either this team had to pass us now or else one of teams would be run off the trail.

I heard the other team pick up speed and Lakota told me that the team was coming up even with us. Lakota told me that the dogs on the other team were in bad shape. I heard the anger in his voice. He did not have to say it, but I knew they were abused.

Doc told us that the musher had a jiggle stick with a strap on it and he was swinging it at Randy! He missed, but took another swipe at Randy's head.

Doc told us that the strap wrapped around Randy's arm. Randy held on to the strap as he yelled, "Banshee". We took off and the sudden jerk of our team pulled the other musher off his sled. Doc told us the trail was narrowing, but soon we were way ahead of the other team. Randy started to slow us down and I thought he was going to stop us so that he could help the other team's dogs. But we heard Musher Stan's voice yell to Randy. "Finish the race. I saw what happened and will take care of Dylan, his team and the missing dog." Fin told us that Musher Stan was driving his team up behind us. He was following us down the trail

Fin and Christmas were doing a fine job of leading. Ugly was telling jokes to the pups and Nitro said, to no dog in particular, "Did you see what Randy did? Now that was a smart move." Yes, it was a very smart move. Randy must have known that the strap would not hurt him since his storm suit would protect him from it. Randy held onto the strap and started to pull on it as he yelled for us to take off down the trail. The sudden forward movement, plus the fact that Dylan was probably off balance on his sled runners, caused Dylan to fall off of his sled.

We entered the finish chute and I heard Mike come up beside the team. "Whoa," Randy called out, telling us to stop. We did, and Fin told me that Mike grabbed the neckline between Fin and Christmas and guided us to our staging spot. I smelled the scent of our truck; it was there waiting to take us home. After the race officials checked out our equipment, I knew Mike or Randy would gave us a snack and some water, before loading us into the dog box to go home.

There was a lot of commotion and I heard that Musher Stan came in with Dylan in his basket and Dylan's sled in tow. Musher Stan talked to Musher GB and told him what had happened on the trail. Musher Stan said that the missing dog was tied into Dylan's team and the missing equipment was in Dylan's sled basket. All of the missing equipment had the owner's name on it.

"Hmmm," said Musher GB, "I think we need the troopers. Sounds like we have a thief. And it looks like he beat these dogs again."

Good, the missing dog was found and the stolen equipment would be retuned to its owner. I was sure that the troopers would take care of Dylan.

After we got our snacks and water, we rested a bit while Randy told Mike about the race. Mike kept telling Randy how smart he was for using the circle, and glad that the magic word helped. Mike told Randy that the dogs looked great after the race and even Doc looked good. "I am glad you pulled him, Randy, I was concerned about him." Mike said.

Then Mike said, "Okay, Let's get these critters back into the dog box and head on home. We have all had enough excitement for a while."

Now, we have a routine for this. Mike or Randy takes off our harnesses and allows us to wander back to the truck. That is, all but me. I walk with Mike, right by his side. He gives me commands so I do not bump into anything. I knew Randy would let Nitro and Lakota go next. Remember, we have a routine.

"Where is that punk that pulled my boy off his sled? I want to teach him a lesson," a voice yelled.

We all stopped. Lakota told me that a very big human was blocking Mike's way to the truck. Nitro told Lakota to stay with him beside Randy, in case this human wanted to harm Randy.

Christmas told me that the man had a knife, and to be careful.

Mike nudged me with his knee as he moved back a step or two. This was trouble.

"Who are you?" Mike asked with a lot of calmness in his voice.

"I am Rufus Crawford, Dylan's dad, and I want to teach that punk a lesson."

"Mister Crawford," Mike said, "I do not believe you are going to teach anyone a lesson right now, especially that boy you keep referring to as a punk. I heard that your boy stole a dog and some equipment and was beating his dogs on the trail. Dylan attacked the boy by my sled and that boy only protected himself. I also understand that your boy is a lot bigger and older than the boy by my sled."

"Lies, lies," Mister Crawford said as he pushed Mike down. I jumped up to protect Mike and felt the knife slash me. I went down.

"Rivers!" Mike yelled as I heard Nitro and Lakota charge Mister Crawford. Christmas told me as I was laying in the snow that Nitro grabbed the hand with the knife in it so, Mister Crawford could not slash out with it, and Lakota knocked Mister Crawford down into the snow. Christmas told me that Lakota then put one of his big paws by Mister Crawford's throat and growled at the human. I could picture this in my mind. The human looking up into the face of a very big, growling and sneering dog who was very upset. I guess that is why the human stopped moving. Of course, having another very big, powerful and upset dog clamped down on your wrist does not leave you too much choice, does it?

I felt Mike's hand on the wound, pressing a cloth over it. I did not think it was too bad. I did not feel any pain. "Randy, please bring me the first aid kit," Mike said.

"I already have it, Mister Mike," Randy answered

I heard Randy kneel down beside me and start to help Mike.

"What happened here, Mike? It was Musher GB. Mister Crawford started to talk and said that the dogs attacked him and he only used the knife to protect himself.

"Not so." It was Musher Stan. "I saw the entire thing. Mister Crawford pushed Mike down and slashed Rivers. The other dogs

acted to protect Mike and Rivers. Look, neither dog has bit Mister Crawford. If they had attacked him, would they be acting the way they are acting now? One has the knife hand and the other is sitting on his chest. Sure don't look like a dog attack to me."

I heard two more sets of footsteps approach and a familiar voice. "Mike, you need help?" It was Doctor Jim.

"Yes, Rivers was slashed by Mister Crawford. I do not think it is bad, but Rivers is bleeding a lot," Mike said.

"Here," Doctor Jim said. "Let me look at him. Nope, it is not too bad, but it needs a couple of stitches. It looks like it was a glancing blow. Bet this is one time Rivers was lucky to be blind. Since Rivers could not see the knife, he probably misjudged his jump. I can fix him up right here." I felt Doctor Jim start to work on my wound.

Another voice spoke up. "I am Trooper Dan Martin. Looks like you had some excitement here. Who wants to start telling me what is going on?"

"I will," said Mister Crawford, "just get these attack dogs off me."

Trooper Martin said. "I think I want you to stay right where you are, sir. You have a knife in your hand and until I am ready to take it from you, that dog is doing a great job. My suggestion to you, sir, is to keep still."

"Son," Trooper Martin said to Randy, "can you tell me what happened?"

Randy told his side of the story, starting with the encounter he had with Mister Crawford's son Dylan out on the trail.

Musher Stan started to talk after Randy finished. "I saw it all, Trooper Martin, both on the trail, where Dylan started to hit Randy with a jiggle stick and then here, when Mister Crawford pushed Mike down and slashed at Rivers. Rivers was protecting Mike, who has a broken arm, and the two dogs on Mister Crawford were protecting Randy. I heard Mister Crawford yell at Mike that he wanted to teach Randy a lesson."

"Mike," Trooper Martin asked, "What do you have to say about this?"

"Nothing much that I could add, Trooper Martin. Stan and Randy pretty much summed it up. Mister Crawford threatened to harm Randy and I was not going to allow that to happen. Mister Crawford pushed me down as I blocked him from getting to Randy. That is when Rivers, who is blind, jumped up to protect me. Mister Crawford slashed at him and Rivers went down.

The other two dogs were protecting Randy. I can assure you that if those two dogs were vicious or not under my control, Mister Crawford would be in very bad shape at this time. As you can see, Mister Crawford's hand still holds the knife, yet there is no blood where my dog has grabbed him."

Trooper Martin asked. "Will your dogs hurt me if I take that knife from Mister Crawford?"

"No," Mike replied.

"Mister Crawford," Trooper Martin said, "I want you to let go of that knife. After I have the knife, the dogs will back off and you will get up. I strongly suggest that you do not make any rash moves. Do you understand?"

"Yes," Mister Crawford snarled. "Get these attack dogs off me."

Christmas told me that Trooper Martin picked the knife up, and Mike told Nitro and Lakota to go back to the team and sit. They did that.

When Mister Crawford got to his feet, Trooper Martin told him that he was under arrest, and asked him to put his hands behind his back.

"When do I get to tell my side of the story?" Mister Crawford demanded.

"You can tell it to the judge. I am arresting you for assault with a deadly weapon, threatening a minor and attacking the dog that you slashed." Trooper Martin replied

"Wait a minute, I was defending my kid, because that Randy kid attacked him on the trail," Mister Crawford yelled.

"Mister Crawford, I have your son Dylan under arrest for assault, dog theft and larceny, plus dog brutality. He confessed to all of the charges. By the way, when I ran his name against our computer, I noticed several outstanding warrants for his arrest for theft and truancy. Mister Crawford, there are several outstanding warrants for you also. With those warrants, plus what you have done here today, and with the testimony of these witnesses, you and your son may be going to jail for a long time. Let's go."

Rest, Recuperation And Surprises

What an adventure this was for Christmas and her pups in their first race! When we got home, and settled, Mary had a big pot of great chow ready for us. She was concerned that I was hurt, but soon realized that I would be okay.

The pups made a big fuss over my stitches, and called me a hero. No, I told them, I only did what I was born to do, take care of my musher, and protect my human buddy. The real heroes were Nitro and Lakota. They risked their lives to protect Randy. Once Mister Crawford knocked Mike down, they were all that stood between Mister Crawford and Randy. Nitro and Lakota surprised me. They could have seriously hurt Mister Crawford, but only used enough force to stop him from harming Randy, or the rest of the team. Who would have thought that those two dogs would do such a brave thing? I know that Sandy, our Guardian Angel Dog, was helping us and guiding us to do the right things, the smart things. Maybe our team believes after all.

Mike and Randy came out of the big house. They were in the kennel and Randy was saying goodbye to us. He told us that it was time for him to get back to his foster home. We were all sad that he had to leave. Yes, we knew he would be back, but....

"What is your rush, Randy"? Mike asked.

"Well, Mister Mike, I have some chores to do and I have to get ready for school. Besides, I want to start writing a story about my first race with the team," Randy said.

Mike replied, "I guess in all the excitement, you forgot that there is no school tomorrow. It is a holiday."

"You are right, Mister Mike, I forgot all about that. However, I still have chores to do," Randy said.

"I am sure you do." Mike said, "But why don't you sit with me

and the dogs for a spell? I am sure they would love to heap some TLC on you. Besides I have something I want you to read."

Now this was getting interesting. We all gathered around Randy and Mike. Stormy told me that Mike pulled a folded piece of paper out of his pocket and gave it to Randy. Randy unfolded the paper and started to read it.

"Would you please read it out loud, Randy? We know you read to the pups when they could not go on the trail. That was very smart of you, because practicing makes you better at something."

"Uh, okay, Mister Mike," Randy said, but I noticed the hesitation in his voice. Stormy told me that Sky went over to where Randy was sitting, sat next to him and gently howled two times. I knew Randy could not understand Sky, but Sky was howling encouragement to Randy. "You can do this, Randy, just read to Mike as you read to Stormy, Tundra and me."

"And Randy," Mike added, "Mike or Mary works. You can drop the Mister or Ms. We are your friends and hope you are ours."

I bet that caught Randy off guard. He started to read in a clear voice. He read all of the words and did not stumble over any of them.

When Randy finished reading the paper, Stormy told me that Mike put his arm around Randy's shoulders and asked him if he understood what the paper meant.

"Yes Mike, it stated that you and Mary want to be my new foster parents."

"That is correct, and you will notice that your old foster parents already have signed the paper agreeing to that. All that is left is for you to agree to that also. What do you say?" Mike asked.

What a shocker this was. Here was a young boy who we met in town a while back and … Oh, you want to know the answer. As Christmas would tell you, it is a no-brainer!!

"When can I move in?" Randy asked.

"Right now," Mike answered. "Mary moved your stuff while you were on the trail."

Afterthoughts

Several nights later, I was sitting in my corner of the yard seeing the sunset in my mind's eye. I was healing fast, and Randy was one happy young musher since he moved in with us. He got his forever home. Caitlyn also got her forever home, and we now had one big family. Yes, Fin joined us also, and Doc recovered completely.

Christmas told me that her pups were getting big and strong. They just loved to run and soon would start lead dog training. Doc had already started working with Tundra, or Tunny, as he affectionately called her.

Sunny visited often, and when she did, we split into two teams and race each other.

One team usually had Christmas and her pups plus Sunny and Fin, while we retired racers made up the second team. Leave it to Sky to come up with our team names: "Fin's Dashing Darlings" and "Doc's Old Geezers." Who wins, you ask? We do not keep track because it is all for fun.

I was thinking about how nice this adventure had turned out when I heard her sit down next to me. "Sandy?" I asked.

"Yes, Rivers, it is me. I just came to tell you how proud I am of you for protecting Mike," she said. I could tell from her voice that she continues to be devoted to him. I know Mike and Mary miss Sandy. There are times when he clips a leash on me and we walk to the garden where she rests. Sometimes Christmas joins us. We sit for a few minutes in the garden and then return to the kennel. I know Christmas feels closer to her Aunt Sandy when we do that.

"You did the same thing right after my operation, remember? You protected Mike from those two bad dogs that attacked him."

"Yes," Sandy said, "but protecting a well Mike against two dogs is nothing compared to being blind and protecting a hurt Mike against a human with a knife. Nitro and Lakota did not think twice either, about protecting you, Mike and Randy. I am proud of all of you."

"Well, Sandy, you know that since we came here to be with Mike and Mary, our lives have all changed for the best. We were all just kennel dogs, but now we have a forever family, a Guardian Angel Dog, and it seems that every time we run a trail, we have another adventure. Life surely is not boring, is it?"

"No, Rivers, it is not boring and I can tell you that your adventures are just beginning. See ya, Rivey. Take care."

And she was gone.